SPIRIT WOLF

VOID

**Center Point
Large Print**

**This Large Print Book carries the
Seal of Approval of N.A.V.H.**

SPIRIT WOLF

GARY SVEE

Center Point Publishing
Thorndike, Maine

This book is dedicated to
Diane, Darren, Nathan, and Beatrice Svee,
to Diane's family, and to my own.

This Center Point Large Print edition
is published in the year 2005 by arrangement with
Pocket Books, a division of Simon & Schuster, Inc.

Copyright © 1987 by Gary Svee.

The text of this Large Print edition is unabridged. In other
aspects, this book may vary from the original edition. Printed in
Thailand. Set in 16-point Times New Roman type.

ISBN 1-58547-516-5

Library of Congress Cataloging-in-Publication Data

Svee, Gary D., 1943-
    Spirit wolf / Gary Svee.--Center Point large print ed.
      p. cm.
    ISBN 1-58547-516-5 (lib. bdg. : alk. paper)
      1. Wilderness areas--Fiction. 2. Wolf hunting--Fiction. 3. Montana--Fiction.
    4. Wolves--Fiction. 5. Large type books. I. Title.

PS3569.V37S67 2005
813'.54--dc22

                                                                    20040122

AUTHOR'S NOTE

There was a hunt for the killer wolf of the Pryor Mountains early in this century. My father, Sigvart Oluf Svee, was one of the men who gathered to stalk that elusive beast.

This book does not describe that hunt. It is rather an adventure of the mind and spirit.

None of the people who abide within these pages live within the memories or memorabilia of men. But walk the streets of Montana and you will see them, bits and pieces, in the faces of the people you pass.

Step beyond the interstate highways that weave their way under the Big Sky and wait. The blocks of stone, the grass, the trees, and the wind in this book will reveal themselves to you. Perhaps then you will see Spirit Wolf.

Gary Svee

1

The voices were muffled through the cracks of the door that led to his parents' bedroom. He heard his father's deep voice, an unintelligible rumble, punctuated by his mother's alto. He had been awakened by the sound of his own name, Nashua, and he knew it must have been his mother speaking because only she called him that. He had long since become Nash to his father.

They were the focus of his twelve-year-old world, and they were talking about him.

He swung his legs out from under the quilt, patched

together from bits and pieces of worn-out shirts and pants, and dropped his feet to the ice-cold wooden floor. Even in the darkness, he could see the cloud his breath made wafting through the cold air toward the broken window at the front of the cabin.

The fire in the big Majestic range had been banked for the night, and it did little more than take the edge off the cold. By morning the bucket of water by the stove would be caked with ice.

Nash felt a shiver course through his body, and he wrapped his arms around himself as he walked over to the bedroom door to listen.

"Mary, we don't have any choice," his father said. "You know how dry it was last year. We didn't get enough wheat for seed. If we don't have a mild winter, we'll run out of hay, and we can't afford to buy any. We don't have any choice. I know it isn't much, but it's all we've got."

And then his mother's protest. "What if a blizzard comes up? What if one of you gets hurt? Losing the place is one thing, but it isn't as important as keeping you and Nash safe. Surely you can see that."

"We don't have any choice. I'm sorry, but it has to be."

Nash heard a little stir in his parents' bed and then silence, and he walked back to his own already cold blankets.

The boy lay wide-eyed for some time, watching light from the hunter's moon outside skip off the breast of the snow and bounce into the cabin. The light was too soft to reveal much, but there wasn't much to see anyway.

A piano, Mary Brue's only heirloom, stood against the

windowless back wall of the room. When the Brues left Minnesota bound for the homestead in Montana, Mary's mother had given the ornate old upright to her. The gift was an unstated acknowledgment that neither would see the other again.

Mary played beautifully. In Minnesota, the minister of the local Lutheran church had been fond of saying that if he could learn to keep his mouth shut and let Mary praise God with her music, the church would be filled to over-flowing each Sunday. He was probably right, but he was too much in love with the sound of his own voice to ever put his theory to the test.

But now Mary's hands were cracked and calloused with the hard labor of homesteading. One summer after-noon, Nash had surprised his mother at the piano, wringing her hands and weeping. She made Nash promise never to tell Uriah.

The rest of the furnishings were rough-hewn, to fit the rough-hewn home. The house had been a line cabin once, years ago, when Montana was still an open range. Nash remembered the look on his mother's face when she first saw the cabin, and the apology in his father's voice as he said, "I know it isn't much, but we'll fix it up, and it will serve until I can build you something better."

That had been five years ago, and still it was the same cabin, still the rough plank floor, worn smooth by the door and by the stove, and splintered elsewhere. Only the muslin draped from the rafters to catch the dirt that dropped through from the sod roof was new.

There was still laughter in the house, but not as often

as there had been at first.

The boy's shivering stopped. Only his nose, poked out from under the blankets, was cold. The warmth drew him into sleep, still wondering what his mother and father had been talking about.

Nash awakened to the sound of the door on the stove firebox rasping open. He watched as his father took sticks from the kindling bucket by the stove and laid them on the few coals left from the night.

Uriah spoke without looking up.

"Better be getting up, boy. I heard Bess calling from the barn a few minutes ago. She's ready for milking."

Nash reached out from the bed and grabbed his shirt and pants from where they lay on the floor. He slipped his clothes under the covers, hoping to warm them a bit before dressing.

"I'll be right there, Dad. Don't let her start without me."

Uriah chuckled at the private joke, which was a daily ritual between the two of them. He chucked a few more sticks on the fire and stepped to the peg on the wall where his coat and hat were hanging.

"You won't be going to school Monday, maybe all week. I want you to split some more wood for your mother. I'm going to hitch up the wagon and haul some hay for the sheep."

Uriah opened the door and stepped into the darkness.

No school! Ordinarily Nash would have been elated to spend a day home, even if it meant work. But now he was vaguely apprehensive. School was important business, and missing it wasn't taken lightly.

Putting on his boots was like plunging his feet into creek water, and Nash wriggled his toes to give them a little breathing room. Then he lighted the brass kerosene lantern, grabbed the galvanized milk bucket, and stepped outside into a cold that took his breath away. It was unseasonably cold, as though someone had left the door to the Arctic open, letting the icy winds loose to play on the Montana prairie. Uriah was fond of saying that the only thing between the North Pole and Montana was a barbed-wire fence, and it blew down two or three times a year.

But it was warmer away from the wind in the log barn where Bess had spent the night. The Guernsey's body heat and the insulation provided by the hay overhead in the loft kept the barn warmer than the house at night.

"Easy, Bess," Nash said to the milk cow. "And I'll trade you some hay for a bucket of milk."

Nash scrambled up the ladder leading to the loft, talking all the while. Uriah said the sound of a man's voice quieted a cow, and Nash would have recited the Gettysburg Address to the cantankerous beast if it made the milking easier. Nash dropped a couple of forkfuls of hay, then descended and closed the stanchion on the cow's neck when she reached out to take it.

"I don't know what's going on, Bess. I'm not going to school today, so it must be important. Mom doesn't want me to go because it's dangerous."

He let *dangerous* roll off his tongue, savoring the taste of it. Then he sat down, gripping the bucket between his knees, and went to work. *Swish, swish,* the milk streamed into the bucket, leaving a layer of froth on the top. Nash shot a couple of streams of milk at the cats waiting expectantly nearby, and stood, hanging his stool back on the wall. He released the stanchion and turned Bess out into the cold.

The bucket was heavy with Bess's milk, and Nash took on a considerable list as he struggled across the yard, milk sloshing at every step. He dropped the bucket off at the little building that housed the separator. Later, before it froze, Mary would separate the cream, which would be hauled to the Miller place to be put on the milk train for town. Cream and eggs were the family's only cash crops during the winter, and it wouldn't be long before the hens stopped laying and Bess dried up.

The sun was touching the sky in the east, and Nash saw his father in the half-light, pitching hay from the stack by the creek into the family's broad-wheeled grain wagon. Then Nash stumped up on the porch and into the house.

"Call your father. It's time for breakfast."

The cabin was warm now, almost hot, and his mother's face was flushed from standing over the stove.

The color in her cheeks brought out her natural prettiness. She was of about medium height, with straw-colored hair and eyes the color of a cloudless summer sky. Her face was fine-featured, ending in a chin that Uriah always thought should be higher in the air than it was generally carried.

Uriah was taller than average and rangy, with a face too craggy to be handsome topped by a shock of hair about the color of the bunchgrass beneath the snow outside. His blue eyes were flecked with brown and never seemed to rest. Uriah would go unnoticed in a crowd but for his straight back and level, appraising eyes; generally one glance at him would draw a second.

Nash walked to the door, savoring the scents of side-pork, potatoes, eggs, and pancakes as he opened the door a crack and shouted to his father.

"Breakfast is ready."

When Uriah waved, Nash shut the door and walked over to the stove. He took the teakettle full of boiling water to the washstand and mixed it half and half with cold water dipped from a bucket his mother had just gotten from the well. He washed his face and hands and sat down at the table.

Uriah stepped in a minute later, stamping snow from his boots. He washed, and the family sat down to breakfast. They ate in silence, trying to get around as much food as possible before more chores pulled them away. Then Uriah stopped, waiting a moment for the meal to sift into the nooks and crannies of his stomach.

"When I was in town yesterday," Uriah said, "I heard some talk about a bounty hunt in the Pryors. Cattlemen got a bee in their bonnet about killing the last Pryor wolf, and they're willing to pay a five-hundred-dollar bounty to the man who kills him. Your mother and I talked it over last night, and you're coming along with me."

Nash tried hard to keep from grinning, but he lost the fight. "When do we leave?"

"This afternoon. We have to get a couple loads of hay up by the sheep pen so your mother can feed them while we're gone."

The rest of the meal passed in silence, but Nash could

swear that the sound of his heart was booming through the room. He was a little scared and a lot excited all at the same time.

Nash floated through the morning. Everything was so easy, it seemed to be magic. Pitchforks full of hay danced to his touch, and the wagon filled twice with so little effort Nash felt like sprinting over to the creek and back just to take the edge off his excitement.

By noon, the chores were done.

His mother had packed a bag with sidepork, bread, flour, coffee, some leftover stew, and a little penny candy she'd had hidden since the family's last trip to town.

"Get Nell saddled and we'll pack the gear," Uriah told the boy.

Nash's excitement soared again. Nell was a work-horse, no doubt about that. She had feet as big as dinner plates and a roman nose that would bring a snicker from any quarter-horse purist, but she was a good horse. Most important, as long as he was astride her, he was on his own. That was important to Nash.

Pulling the hay wagon had taken the edge off Nell, and she stood patiently while Nash set the bit between her teeth and dropped the old Miles City saddle over her back. Then, more from reflex than malice, Nell sucked in a deep breath when Nash tried to cinch the saddle tight. And more from habit than malice, Nash stepped back and kicked her as hard as he could in the belly. The breath went out of the mare with a *woof,* and Nash pulled the cinch up to the worn spot and buckled it.

By the time Nash was finished, Uriah was tying a burlap bag behind the boy's saddle. They walked together to the house, each leading his horse.

Mary looked up from the stove as the door opened. She stood there, motionless, as though to prolong the moment, to postpone the goodbye.

Uriah busied himself, putting together the final bits and pieces of the supplies he and Nash would need. He seemed very intent on his tasks, too intent to speak, too intent to look into Mary's eyes.

Then, with his pockets stuffed with another handful of matches, more candles, and a few more pieces of jerky, Uriah reached up on the wall and took down the rifle and the shotgun, handing the shotgun to Nash.

Suddenly, Mary was beside Uriah holding his arms, speaking to him so rapidly and softly Nash could barely hear.

"Uriah, the Lazy KT is close to the reservation. You're as apt to bump into Indians as not. . . ."

Her voice hung there, saying nothing, saying everything.

Uriah's face went flat, like a washed-out photograph.

"The best thing for those Indians on the reservation is to stay on the reservation."

"But what if they don't?" she asked, apprehension hanging on her voice like frost on a window.

"That's their lookout." Uriah's voice was low and hard.

Mary stepped into Uriah's arms, holding him to her tightly, protectively. She stood there until the stiffness in Uriah's back and face eased, and then she looked into his eyes.

"Leave it be, Uriah, before it tears you apart."

Uriah shook his head. "I can't. You know I can't."

There was a catch in Mary's voice as she said, "No matter what happens, you come back, and bring Nashua with you."

Then Mary turned to Nash. "You take care of yourself," she said. "Do what your dad tells you. Stay warm and don't get too tired. The wolf isn't as important as you are. Remember that."

Nash couldn't remember the last time his mother had hugged him. She'd stopped doing it, he thought, in a tacit recognition that he was growing up, but she hugged him now, bending only a little to reach him.

Mary followed Uriah and Nash to the door.

"Be careful," she said as they stepped outside to the horses, hesitating a moment before mounting.

Nash looked back minutes later just before he nudged Nell into the creek ford. His mother was still standing in the doorway, a touch of color against the drabness that was the cabin.

Uriah stopped on the other side of the creek. "We'll stay at the Andersons' tonight. We should get there about dark."

It was cold enough to paint breath against air as clear as a prism. Anything dark stood out so sharply against the snow it appeared etched on the mind.

As the two passed, the only sounds were the caws of magpies perched in the cottonwoods and the singing of the snow underfoot.

Uriah had slipped his rifle into the scabbard that hugged his horse's side. Nash balanced the family's twelve-gauge double-barreled shotgun with Damascus barrels over Nell's neck. Nash had hunted rabbits and birds with the shotgun before, but only halfheartedly. The weapon had a wicked kick and the knife-edged stock dropped so sharply the shooter knew he put his cheekbone in jeopardy every time he squeezed the trigger. Nash's respect for the double-barrel was so great he fired it only when, in his excitement, he forgot the consequences of squeezing the trigger. The gun was empty. His father carried the shells, double-ought buck-shot, in his saddlebags.

"Not many people are accidentally shot with an empty gun," he explained.

Uriah's rifle was a lever-action Winchester, a deer killer. Antelope and deer. Staples. Nature's meat market.

Nash remembered beefsteak from family meals in Minnesota. But there was no beefsteak in Montana. Deer steak hammered tender and coated with flour to take away the taste of sage and willow and wont. Beef, if you had beef, was for market. Venison was for the table.

Nash had killed his first deer that fall after the weather cooled enough to keep the meat until it aged. It was a dry doe. The rifle put her down, backbroken.

Nash walked toward the stricken deer. She was struggling to pull herself to safety, but her back legs wouldn't work. They dragged uselessly behind her like anchors. As Nash neared, she stopped struggling and turned to look at this man-creature who was killing her. Nash lifted the rifle to fire a bullet through her brain, to close those eyes that looked at him with such fear and wonder, but Uriah pushed the rifle aside. Bullets, like everything else, were too precious to waste.

The doe struggled again as Uriah approached. He straddled her, cradling her neck almost gently in his left arm. Then he began sawing at her throat with a knife honed to razor sharpness. Nash watched and listened to the doe bleat as the knife sought her lifeblood. Then the knife found her windpipe, and the only sound was her gasping breath, until the life drained out of her and her head sank to the ground.

And Uriah looked at Nash then, handing him the bloodied knife.

"Time you learned."

Uriah grabbed a hind leg and held the deer open to Nash. The knife cut through hide and tissue to the body cavity below, and the smell came then, the smell of life and death emanating from the deer's guts and rising into the cold air. Nash cut the anus free and then sliced around the diaphragm, as he had seen his father do dozens of times. Then, holding his breath against the stench, he reached his arm deep into the deer's body and grasped her esophagus with his hand. He braced his legs and tugged until the windpipe tore free and the deer's guts spilled on the ground.

Nash ate meat from that deer, but never without seeing in his mind's eye that river of guts spilling on the ground. And he never again pointed a gun at game without seeing the look in that doe's eyes as his father cut her throat.

The horses were plowing through drifts caught in the lee of a little rise and their breath plumed up like smoke from a locomotive laboring up a hill.

Nash had been on only one train trip in his life, but he

would never forget it. All the family's possessions—furniture, stock, tools—were loaded into a single "immigrant" car, the Brues into a hard-riding, smoke-filled passenger car. His mother had packed food to eat on the way, and the Brue family jolted, lurched, and jerked along for a thousand miles, passing the time at each stop feeding the stock and cleaning out their car. His father spent most of his time in the stockcar, peering out the crack in the door when he wasn't busy.

It was spring then, and emerald grass painted the prairies a pale green. Fields of wildflowers fled past the windows in startling bursts of color. The family thought the prairie was paradise then. Land that didn't have to be cleared to be plowed. Grass knee high stretched as far as the eye could see. They were playing a part in a story of high adventure and their excitement grew with each passing mile.

And then there was Billings, a little town walled between massive rimrocks overlooking the Yellowstone River. Uriah bought a newspaper there. The city was destined to grow, "farsighted" businessmen said. It was blessed with good water, good land, and good people. An Indian had been cut to pieces under the wheels of a train. A hue and cry from the city's saloon owners followed the sheriff's conjecture that the Indian was drunk. No white man would serve an Indian liquor. No sir!

They switched trains in Laurel, heading south toward Wyoming. Finally they were in Bridger, unloading the immigrant car, free of the smoky confines of the train. Then came the ride to the homestead in the rattly, rough-riding wagon. Nash had never been so excited.

A few weeks later the family discovered that green was a rare and fleeting thing on the Montana prairie. The land scorched brown, mottled only by the color clinging to springs, creeks, and rivers.

Nell was laboring by the time they reached the top of the hill, and his father reined his roan to a stop.

"Not good to get them heated in weather like this."

Nash climbed down and stretched his legs. "How much farther to the Andersons'?"

"Not far now. We'll be there by dark."

About halfway across the flat, the man and the boy came to the road that tied their farm to the Andersons' and the homesteads of the dozen other families that had homesteaded along the foothills. It was easier going then, and Nell settled into a rocking, mile-eating gait. Nash fell into a half sleep, jerked awake as they pulled the horses to a stop on the edge of the Anderson homestead.

The Anderson place was frame lumber, black, with a layer of tar paper. Most places it would have been called a tar-paper shack. On the endless plains of Montana, it was called home. Lars was down by the creek, breaking ice to water his stock. Nash and Uriah saw him stop and wipe his face with a red bandana. He looked up as he felt the newcomers' eyes on him. Anderson studied Nash and Uriah for a moment, his memory sifting through horses and the way men sat them before he came up with their names. Then he stuck his arm into the air and waved them in.

Lars Anderson was grinning as they rode up.

"Well, I didn't expect to see you here, Uriah, Nash. But you're welcome. Climb down. Edna will have dinner ready in a bit. You have to stay with us tonight, you know. Too late to go anywhere else."

"Thank you, Lars. We'll take you up on that. We'll give you a hand with the chores."

It was all ritual: the invitation, the acceptance, and the offer to help with the chores were a bit of prairie etiquette as rigid as the protocol of any eastern drawing room.

Lars was slight, of medium height; his ordinary kind of face—save for the icy blue eyes and the constant grin—topped by a shock of brown hair. He was the kind of man people described as wiry, and maybe a little electric, too. When he talked, his arms fluttered through the air as though he were trying to keep his balance on a high wire.

"Uriah, you're looking a little peaked. Yes sir, you're looking a little peaked."

"Now that you mention it, I've been feeling a little peaked," Uriah answered with a grin. "Just don't know what to do about it."

For a man who looked "a little peaked," his father had an odd air of expectancy, Nash thought, and a moment later he learned why.

"I've got just the thing for you. Picked it up a couple of weeks ago in town. It's about as good a cure for what ails you as anything I've found. We have to go to the barn anyway to put the horses away, so I'll let you try some."

"Well, thank you, Lars. I'll just take you up on that."

They walked to the barn, leading the horses. The

building was wholly unremarkable. Like most on Montana homesteads, it was built to make do until better times. The structure the little group stepped into was more shed than barn, but it offered some shelter.

Nash and his father slipped the saddles off the horses and rubbed the tired animals down. Meanwhile, Lars tossed a few forkfuls of hay to the horses. When the tasks were done, Lars reached above the doorframe and pulled down a bottle of whiskey. "I'm not sure what dosage you're supposed to take, but a good, long pull or two seems to do me a lot of good."

His words were followed by the sound of a popping cork and the smell of whiskey. Lars passed the bottle to Uriah, and Uriah took a long drink. His face worked for a moment, tears filling his eyes as the raw whiskey burned his throat. But when he passed the bottle back to Lars, there was a grin on his face.

Lars took another long pull at the bottle, and his face flushed pink. He passed the bottle back to Uriah.

Uriah took another drink and winked at Nash as he handed the bottle to Lars. Lars managed to take a long swallow with only a slight grimace.

Uriah held up his hands when Lars tried to hand him the bottle again.

"That's all for me, Lars. Wouldn't do for me to drink any more before I see Edna. You know how those women are. Mary would be colder than an outhouse in a snowstorm if I showed up in my cups at one of her friends' homes."

"Aye. And I wouldn't have to wait long to pay penance for my part in it either," Lars said. "About the time you two stepped out of the door, Edna would be out here poking around for my bottle. Women just don't understand how taking a drink now and then picks up a man's spirits."

"Well, your spirits picked me up considerable," Uriah said, and the men roared. The whiskey worked fast on empty stomachs and both were humming as they walked up to the house.

They were met along the way by the younger Anderson kids, John, Elizabeth, and Joanne.

"What are you kids doing hanging back like that? You know the Brues. Now go tell your mother and Ettie that we have company for the night." The three drifted off like snow riding a cold wind.

Ettie was the only student Nash's age in the Lone Pine School. They were as close as girls and boys can be in that awkward time between childhood and adulthood. She was pretty, like her mother, and when puberty took the hard edges off her, she would be close to beautiful. Nash wasn't really aware of that, nor did he ever wonder why when the cold was trying to steal the warmth from his bed he sometimes found himself thinking about her.

Ettie was setting the table as her father and the two visitors came through the door. She glanced up, smiled, and went back to her work. Edna stepped away from the stove.

"You two know you're always welcome here. Wash up and sit down at the table. I want to hear about Mary, and what brings the two of you out in weather like this."

Edna was a little taller than her husband, light-complexioned like him, but more serious. Not stern, just

21

serious. Lars said it was his job to plow and pitch hay, and it was Edna's job to take care of the kids and worry. She accomplished both tasks with great style.

Lars said grace amid the twittering of the younger children, and they all settled down to eat. There was stew—chunks of venison steaming in a mixture of potatoes and carrots—set off with bread fresh from the oven and covered with slabs of melting homemade butter.

While they ate, Uriah told the Andersons about the Pryor wolf, the contest, and the five hundred dollars.

Uriah had just put a period on his last sentence when Lars stepped in to pick up the story.

"Some folks," Lars said in a hushed, conspiratorial voice, "say the Pryor wolf is a ghost that roams the prairie in the dark of the moon."

Lars's voice dropped to a whisper. The children leaned forward in their chairs to listen to him, to hear this story whispered in the dim light of a kerosene lamp.

"And when it's dark, so dark you can't see your breath on the night air, so dark you don't know if you are alive or dead, you can see his eyes burning like two coals, searching the prairie for LITTLE GIRLS AND BOYS TO EAT!"

He ended the story with a hard slap on the table, and every child, Nash included, jumped.

Lars whooped, and Edna grinned, trying to sound stern as she said, "Lars, you're going to scare these kids so bad they won't be able to sleep."

Nash's ears were burning. He hoped Ettie hadn't noticed how he had jumped at the slap. Imagine a wolf hunter jumping at a little trick like that.

Lars grinned at Edna. "The kids know well enough by now to take their papa with a grain of salt," he said. Then he turned to Uriah. "Smart to take Nash along. He can be a big help in the camp while you're out hunting."

"Nash will be hunting with me," Uriah replied.

Lars looked at Uriah, hesitating a moment before he continued. "Uriah, I've heard stories about this wolf, stories I wouldn't tell the children. Stories I wish I hadn't heard."

"I've heard those stories, too, but you know as well as I do that if you get a bunch around a campfire, there'll be more stories than smoke in the air. Ghost wolf! Grown men pass that story around like it was gospel. This wolf is something special, all right, but he's no more ghost than I am."

Then Uriah slapped the table, but nobody jumped, nobody laughed.

Lars leaned forward, into the ball of yellow light cast by the kerosene lamp. "Uriah, I saw Zeke Campbell's little herd of cattle after that wolf finished with them. They were all bunched up against a fence in a spring storm, cows and calves. That wolf killed them all. I won't tell you how he killed them. I don't want that on my kids' minds like it is on mine, some nights when I'm out in the dark and I hear the dogs barking and I don't know why. But I'll tell you there was something evil got into those cattle that night, something I wouldn't ever want to meet."

Uriah was silent, but Nash probably wouldn't have heard him if he had spoken. His thoughts were racing through what he had heard at the table tonight.

Ghost wolf! Nash pretended that it made no difference to him whether he was hunting a ghost or not, but his effort was sickly at best. He picked at his food through dinner, hearing only snatches of conversation at the table.

When the last plate was empty and the last stomach filled, Ettie and Edna began clearing the table. Lars, stretching in his kitchen chair, said to Uriah, "Let's get a breath of fresh air. It's a little stuffy in here."

Uriah nodded, and the two men stepped outside. If they were really looking for fresh air, they found it. The temperature had dropped with the sun, and the wind was picking up. Little drifts of snow were marching across the pasture, growing and shrinking under the artistry of the wind. It was cold, and the men's ears popped in the occasional gusts.

"You're looking a little peaked, Uriah," Lars said. "I've got just the thing for you." Uriah laughed and followed Lars to the barn.

Inside the cabin, Nash offered to help with the dishes, but he was turned down. He had grown in stature during dinner, during the talk about the wolf hunt. Ettie's younger brother and sisters stood back from him, as though some magic had transformed him into someone they didn't know and it was not proper to ask him to help with the dishes.

After the dishes were done, Ettie brought out a limp deck of cards, and the children played rummy to a background of hoots and jeers. Edna Anderson sewed, mending socks and stitching patches over patches on the knees of the younger children's denim pants in the light of the kerosene lamp. At about nine thirty she dropped her work into a wicker sewing basket.

"Time for bed" brought a chorus of protest, but that was only a matter of form, part of the nightly ritual of the family.

"Nash, I'll make up a bed for you by the fire. You might throw a stick or two into the stove during the night if you get cold."

The ritual of going to bed, undressing, donning night-shirts, and saying prayers and a parade of good nights took nearly half an hour. After the latch closed on the door to the family's bedrooms, Nash stripped off his clothes and climbed into the pile of quilts stacked on the floor. The bed was comfortable, the room warm, and Nash near exhaustion. It was a matter of moments before he was asleep, and it seemed only moments had passed, too, before he was awakened.

Nash didn't know if it was the sound of the two men whispering or the blast of cold air following them through the open door that awakened him. They were whispering together and twittering. Nash was intrigued and embarrassed at the same time. Imagine grown men—imagine his own father—twittering.

Uriah tossed a stick of wood into the stove, still chuckling to himself, and lay down on the makeshift bed on the floor. It wasn't as easy for Lars. Nash could hear the discussion in the bedroom.

"What in the world have you been doing to keep you out till this time of night? It's nearly midnight."

Lars's voice was slurred, staggering like his walk. "Well, Edna, Uriah was feeling a little peaked, so we've been doctoring."

"You have a bottle again, don't you? You've got one hidden out in the barn somewhere."

"No, Edna. I can swear on a stack of Bibles that there isn't a drop of liquor in the barn. Now go to sleep. I don't feel so good."

Nash heard a muffled *whoof, whoof, whoof* coming from his father's blankets as the boy turned over. Nash whoofed a few times, too, before he went to sleep.

Morning came early, and Nash awakened to the creak of the stove door and the thump of wood tossed on a bed of embers inside. At first he thought he was home, that Uriah would be calling him in a moment to go milk Bess, and then his mind caught up with the morning.

"Better get up, Nash. We've got to get moving."

Nash climbed out into the cold, shivering as he slipped into his wool pants and flannel shirt. He was sitting on the floor pulling on his shoes when Mrs. Anderson came out of the bedroom.

"Lars isn't feeling well this morning," she said, and Nash could have sworn a wink followed her words. "But I told him he should get up and look at his 'patient'."

Uriah smiled, but the expression was almost as much grimace as glee. He seemed pale and his skin a little pasty, but compared to Lars he was the picture of health.

Lars appeared gnomelike from the bedroom. He was bent over as though he were trying to stay below a black cloud hanging over his head. His face seemed swollen and blotchy, eyes hidden in squints, as he wove gingerly across the room.

Uriah's face bent and cracked into a painful grin.

"You're looking a little peaked, Lars," Uriah said. "I've got just the thing for you."

Lars looked up and his face turned stark white. He bolted for the door, shirttail flying, and plummeted through the wall of cold waiting outside as though it didn't exist.

"He didn't have any shoes on," Nash said, but no one was listening.

Uriah was whoofing again, and Edna twittering. Nash was glad his father wasn't twittering anymore.

Lars spent breakfast curled around his coffee, wincing whenever cup clattered against saucer. It was clear it would be a quiet Sunday at the Anderson place.

It was still dark as Uriah saddled their horses and led the two animals from the barn to the house. At Uriah's knock, the Anderson children spilled from the house into a circle of light streaming from the cabin door. Ettie was there, too, hanging back a little by her mother, shoulder set against the doorframe.

"Just wanted to say thanks. You're welcome at our home anytime," Uriah said.

"No thanks needed," answered Edna. "You two come back, and bring Mary next time."

"We'll do that."

They rode away in silence, suspended in the night, in space, with light from the stars striking sparks on the snow until false dawn dulled the dark. The world turned drab before it turned bright, and it did turn bright. The first touch of the sun ignited the night's frost on the snow and set the prairie on fire with a flash of white as cold as death and bright as life.

The horses were frisky, and their riders nudged them into a trot for a mile or two, and then Uriah, his face pale, pulled the animals to a brief stop.

"Are you feeling a little peaked?" Nash asked, and his father broke into laughter, color coming back into his face.

"Try not to be as foolish as your father," Uriah said with a grin. "Isn't anything made better looking at it through the bottom of a bottle."

2

The country was beginning to break up into sharp, pine-fringed coulees outlined by sandstone rimrocks. Sage and yucca poked through the snow, and prickly pear huddled beneath. On ridges exposed to the wind, bunch-grass long since dried into hay tempted the horses to snatch at it in passing.

Here and there man had left his mark on the land; a straggling corral made of lodgepole pine nailed to living trees, an old trapper's soddy caving in under the weight of the land and the years, and now and then a homestead shack with wide-eyed kids watching the two horsemen pass.

The day was bright and clear and the sun gave the illusion of warmth although it was cold enough to numb the hands and feet. Nash and Uriah stopped around the middle of the day and climbed off the horses. Nash was more than a little grateful. He felt stiff and sore, his muscles and bones not yet content with the saddle.

"Won't be long now. We're on the Lazy KT," Uriah

said. "Not more than a couple of miles."

Not long, but it seemed like hours to Nash before they came to the corner post, cut from a giant cottonwood and branded ⊵T, which marked the entrance to the ranch. They rode up a neat barbed wire lane to the ranch house a mile deeper into the hills.

It was a good spread. Anyone who had ever worked the land could see that. Corrals were put into the ground to stay. Stacks of hay put up by men who knew what they were doing poked out of the hay-ground down by the creek, and the barn was one of the biggest structures Nash had seen. It was built of lumber, rough-cut, like most everything else in that country, but it had a real mortar and stone foundation and it put most homes to shame. The other ranch buildings—the tack shed, bunkhouse, and even the sturdy outhouses—lent an air of prosperity to the scene.

As the two pulled into the yard, Katie Jeffries called from the kitchen door of the ranch house.

"Uriah! Nash! Come have a cup of coffee and warm up. Suppose you came here for the hunt. I'll tell you where the doings are."

Uriah and Nash climbed down, loosened the cinches on their saddles, and walked up to the front door.

Katie's mother had died when the girl was ten years old, and she grew wild, like the cattle on the ranch. Women were rare in the territory then, and cowhands were more comfortable with the ladies who spent their evenings in the Stockman's Bar in Billings—and the rooms above—than they were with the boss's daughter. So they treated her like one of the boys, and she came to accept the solitude. She considered herself happy, those years when she was a man-child, happy until her father took her and a load of cattle to Chicago one year. The streets of the Windy City were a rude awakening for the wild girl from Montana. Ladies swirled around the city like animated bouquets of flowers. She watched the other patrons of restaurants and learned how inadequate her bunkhouse manners were. She listened to the lilt of conversations in hotel lobbies and realized how little she knew outside the world of cattle and men and Montana.

And on her return to the ranch she became a voracious reader, reaching out to the world beyond. She worked to improve herself as hard as she worked on the ranch, filling her spare hours with study.

And then she met Ulysses Jeffries. He was a remittance man, profligate son of a rich English family, sent to the American West to save his family from embarrassment. Ulysses Jeffries stood out on the frontier like a daisy in a cactus patch. He was an oddity, a man who talked funny and dressed like a dude. But the stockmen's association recognized that Jeffries was more than that, and sent the Englishman to Helena to lobby the legislature. He held the rough-cut Montanans in thrall with his bearing and clarion voice.

He was on association business when he first met Katie. She had been out checking cattle that day and didn't return until after dinner. Ulysses and Katie's father were sitting in the kitchen-livingroom-parlor of their three-room cabin when Katie stepped through the door. Ulysses looked up and kept looking.

Katie was burned brown by the spring sun, and she

smelled more of horse than anything else, but Ulysses noticed something no one else had. Katie was a woman, and a pretty one at that.

Katie couldn't keep her eyes and ears off the stranger. As they were introduced, Ulysses took her hand and kissed it, and a flush of pink crept under the deep tan of Katie's face.

She was embarrassed, elated, and flustered all at the same time, and the best she could manage in response was "I declare," a line straight from a book she was reading on the prewar South. And when he looked at her and grinned, she fled from the room—but not far and not fast.

Their courtship was a strange affair, neither being sure what was proper in the other's world, but both so determined that it would work that it did.

As Uriah and Nash entered the kitchen, Katie said, "Come in. Come in. I've got some hot coffee waiting. You want coffee or cocoa, Nash?"

"Cocoa, please."

"That's a good choice," Katie said. "I believe I'll have some too."

Nash's hands were still a little numb from the ride, and he stood in front of the coal-burning range in the kitchen, palms out, reaching for the heat.

"You should have brought Mary. We could have sent a man over to your place to feed the sheep. I would have liked the company. People are thicker than hairs on a dog's hind leg around here, and about as much fun to talk to, at least until you two came along."

She turned from stirring the cocoa on the stove and

gave Nash a wink.

The cocoa was hot enough to burn Nash's lip as he took his first sip, but he savored the rare treat, holding the cup near his face so he could feel its heat and smell the chocolate.

"Ulysses drew quite a crowd. They're down by the old cabin. Some of them started coming in a couple of days ago. Wanted to do some scouting before the rest showed up, but Ulysses put a stop to that. That man's got a sense of the dramatic. By the time this thing starts, he'll have the whole crowd straining at the tether, all for an old wolf. Funny, but I'll be sorry to see the old wolf go. He's as much a part of this ranch as I am.

"Sorry to chatter on so, but I don't get much chance to visit. How is everything with the Brue family?"

"Pretty good," Uriah said. "We're short on hay. Looks like our milk cow is about to dry up. The sheep are bunching up in the cold, and two of them have suffocated already." Uriah let out a snort. "Pretty good, I'd say."

Katie laughed too.

"You'll make a Montanan yet," she said. "I knew you would the first time I saw you."

Uriah turned serious. "It was a tough year. Dry. But I'm going to try to put in a ditch next summer. If I can irrigate the meadow, I can triple my hay tonnage. Maybe add a few head of cattle. Put in a little barley, too."

"That's what Ulysses says too. Irrigation is the answer for country like this. Want you to know that we can help out if you need it. We'd like to have a good steady source of hay. You could pay us back that way."

Uriah stiffened a little in his chair.

"Didn't ask for charity," he said.

"Didn't offer it," Katie answered. "In case you didn't notice, we were talking business."

Katie bustled back to the stove for the large enameled coffeepot and poured Uriah another cup. "No need to be so sensitive. We want good neighbors out here. You and Mary and Nash are good neighbors."

The front legs of Uriah's chair bumped back on the hardwood kitchen floor. "Sorry. I didn't mean to give offense."

"None taken. Nash, how's school going this year? Who's getting the best grades, you or that pretty Anderson girl, Ettie?"

"We're pretty much even," Nash said. He and Ettie had indeed been competing for grades over the past years. The competition spurred them along, and pulled them together, too.

"You better take your horses out to the barn. Tell Bill I said to give them oats and a rubdown. You're going to have a hard time for the next few days and you don't want your horses to give out. Ulysses is going to start the whole thing in about fifteen minutes. You better walk down there and listen to him. He'll be upset if you don't. You know how he never misses an opportunity to give a speech, and he's got his hooks into that bunch out there. They have to listen to him if they want a chance at the bounty. You stop in on your way back out. Spend the night here before you go. No sense taking a chance on the weather."

"We might do that, Katie. Thank you for the coffee and

cocoa. We'll be going now."

"Now, you stop in before you go home. Remember," Katie called after them as they walked to the hitching rail where their horses were waiting.

They led the animals over to the barn, glad for the chance to stretch the muscles in their legs. Bill took over from there while Uriah and Nash walked over a small knoll to the old ranch sprawled in a meadow below. The meadow was carpeted with people—moving, chattering, foot-stomping people. They were a mixed group; ranchers and homesteaders in abundance, and a sprinkling of men who preyed on other men's weaknesses. Dudes poked out of the crowd here and there, but Nash was most fascinated by the hunters and trappers. Some of the bearded, fur-bedecked men were of an age to have been buffalo hunters. Some of them had been. They were men who took their lives from death, and their faces showed that.

Just beyond the crowd was a wagon parked against one of the old outbuildings. Standing near that wagon was Ulysses Jeffries.

Ulysses was easy to spot. He collected stares as casually as a child on an outing collects stones. There was something about his bearing that pulled men's eyes and conjecture to him. Ulysses looked up as Uriah and Nash strode down the hill, and lifted his arm in welcome.

It was time. The introduction was given by one of the neighboring ranchers. Uriah and Nash arrived at the edge of the crowd. The Englishman-turned-Montanan climbed gracefully into the bed of the wagon and stood there silently for a moment, waiting for the sheer weight of his presence to capture the attention of the crowd. It did. Quiet bumped against noise until all was silent.

At that moment, Ulysses began to speak. "Gentlemen," he said in a voice that seemed somehow too heavy for his tall lean body. "Gentlemen," Ulysses repeated. "There are some one hundred twenty souls gathered here today, a bigger turnout than any of us expected, and that will work in your favor. Perhaps you can do what nobody else has been able to. Perhaps the sheer weight of your numbers will allow you to succeed where all others have failed. That is what we, members of the Montana Cattlemen's Association, are hoping. We hope, once and for all, to be rid of this scourge that has plagued us for so long.

"Most ranchers would understand the loss of a calf now and then to wildlife. It is the natural order of things that predators kill to eat. Our cultivation of animals obeys that order. But this wolf kills for pleasure.

"If you had come, as those of us who live in this area have, to a meadow strewn thick with the carcasses of newborn calves, you would hate this animal as we do.

"He is a piece of the past, a beast of another time that leaves his scat where we tread. He must be killed. He must be killed to make way for us.

"The cattlemen of Montana have carved the future from the dirt and rocks and grass and trees and water of this place. The gold miners have taken their gold and gone. The buffalo hunters have killed the buffalo and gone. Only we remain, we and the homesteaders who are coming after us.

"We have met each challenge head on—and beaten it.

When rustlers were thicker on the plains of eastern Montana than the cattle they stole, cattlemen rented a train and loaded it with men, horses, gear and rope. Each time the men on that train came across a rustler, they left him dangling from the nearest tree, like a crow strung up on a fence to frighten other crows away. We were the law then because there was no other. We did what had to be done to make this country safe.

"And bandits were the least of what we faced. At first, there were the Indians. They would come to the doors of our ranch houses, and if the man was gone—if the odds were right for their particular brand of courage—they would rape and kill the women and steal the children.

"And even these, these noble savages we have read about in dime novels written by men who have never ventured farther west than the Mississippi, were nothing compared to this land.

"It writhes like a snake under man's touch. In the summer, winds from the deserts of the world are turned back by the blasts of air that sear these plains and hide the horizon behind a veil of shimmering heat. The summer wind sucks the soil dry and then picks it up and carries it like a blast of shot from a double-barrel into the face of man or beast who ventures out on these god-forsaken plains.

"And summers, those dry, hot, miserable summers, are paradise compared to the time when winter has its way on the prairie. It is cold today. The thermometer outside our kitchen window, or what remains of the window under winter's layer of frost, records today's temperature as twenty degrees below zero. It is twenty degrees below zero, and you and I stand here talking as though it were a balmy spring day."

Nash was transfixed by Ulysses's words, carried along by them, a leaf in a windstorm, but he was brought abruptly to the ground by the sound of a nearby voice.

"That man's as full of crap as a Christmas goose," the voice said. "If it's balmy today, it's because of all that hot air that old geezer is spewing out."

The voice came from a rough-looking character with a full, black beard and a derby hat. He was dressed more city than country, with a heavy coat worn more from the rub of bar tops than from work. Had he been a baby, a doting mother would have referred to him as pleasingly plump. As a man, he somehow seemed too soft.

"I thought we came here to kill a wolf, not to be jawed to death by that old bastard," he said, and he glanced at a man standing next to him as though for approval.

The second man was leaner, dressed more like the cowhands around him, and almost invisible to the crowd. Nash couldn't see the second man's face. It was hidden under the brim of a down-turned Stetson.

The second man said nothing, but the hat brim canted up a moment to reveal the hidden eyes to his burly companion.

Whatever the man saw in those eyes caused him to recoil as though he had been slapped. He shuffled his feet a moment and was silent.

". . . Most of you don't remember the winter of eighty-six. Most of you weren't in Montana yet. Some of you weren't yet born," Ulysses said with a nod in Nash's direction. "But those of us who were in Montana then will never forget it. The winds screamed out of Canada like souls of the possessed, and they carried with them snow that bit your face white. The cattle moved ahead of that storm, drifting with the wind until they came up to a coulee or a rimrock or a river. Then they stood with that wind to their backs while the snow covered them.

"The cattle froze standing up and they stayed that way until spring when the snows melted. Then they rotted from the outside in. Cattlemen tried to stop the awful slaughter. They fought that wind as though it were another man, a rustler or a wild Indian. They might as well have fought death. Their bodies were found the next spring too. Along the lower Yellowstone only one cow in ten lived through that winter. In all, some three hundred sixty-two thousand head of cattle perished—nearly sixty percent of all the cattle in the state.

"And the open range died with the cattle. Ranchers changed, philosophies changed, and modern ranching was born from that time when hell came to this state.

"We have lived through hard times. Through the cold of winter. Through drought and floods and fire and hail, but, by God, we lived!

"This wolf is a reminder of the past. The stink of it curls the nostrils of decent men. It is a symbol of all that we want to leave behind. And we want its head. We want it grinning down from the wall of the stockmen's headquarters in Miles City.

"That is all that I have to say. My foreman will explain the rules to you. May the best man bring that beast to ground. Thank you for your attention, gentlemen."

Ulysses's foreman was tall and rangy and sported a

mustache flecked with gray. He was not accustomed to speaking to large groups of people, and his nervousness soon became apparent in the way he shuffled his feet and stumbled over the words. But it was just as obvious that he was a man accustomed to giving orders.

"Everybody to the left of my arm take about ten steps to your left," he said, and he moved through the crowd like that, dividing the men into five groups. Then he climbed up on the wagon seat.

"Nobody has seen the wolf for years, but we find his kills scattered all over. We're going to send you to one of five camps. Just so you know that we're not trying to give anybody an edge, one man from each group will pick the name of the camp out of my hat."

In turn men stepped forward and took pieces of paper from the foreman's Stetson: Spring Creek, Horseman Meadow, Cowboy Steele Flat.

Nash and his father were in the fourth group, and as the foreman moved toward them, the heavyset man who had been criticizing Ulysses during his speech grabbed Nash by the arm.

"The kid will draw for us," he said, and he shoved Nash toward the foreman. Nash stumbled forward, afraid to be the center of attention, afraid to retreat into the anonymity of the crowd. He reached into the hat and handed the foreman a folded piece of paper.

"This bunch is on Dry Creek," the foreman announced, holding the paper out at arm's length to read it. "Jack Flynn will take you out there. We've got a man in each camp to act as the association's representative. If you have any questions, you can ask him. Jack, you step out here so they can see you."

Flynn was a man in his late sixties. A shock of gray hair fanned out from a ruddy face wrinkled like the land where he had spent most of his time. He had what Uriah called "whiskey eyes," eyes dimmed from the rotgut that passed for bourbon in the West of earlier times. But he wasn't a bum, and there were more laugh lines than frowns cut into his face. He tipped his hat to the group, and his face crinkled into a grin.

"Pleased to be of service," he said, with a faint touch of Old Eire in his voice.

The foreman's voice pulled their attention back to the wagon. "You people are going to be a half day's ride from here. You're going to be a long way from help if you get in trouble, so don't get in trouble. The barometer has been rising, so you should get decent weather, but you all know how quick that can change. Ol' Doc has promised to stay here at the ranch for the week this thing is goin' on. He'll do what he can if somebody gets hurt. We got oats and hay for the horses at the camps. Your grub is up to you. Good luck."

As Nash turned, he saw his father talking to the stranger who had shoved Nash. The stranger was grinning, but Uriah was not. Taller and slighter, Uriah seemed to be leaning on the column of air that separated the two men. As Nash drew nearer, Uriah stepped away, and the stranger chuckled. But there was no humor in the laugh, only malevolence.

The crowd was milling around, the men shouting directions, encouragement, and strategy at each other. Already conjecture had begun about which camp would likely claim the prize. Nash and Uriah walked through the men to where Ulysses was standing.

"That was some speech, Ulysses. Made the hair stand up on the back of my neck."

"Wasn't meant to do that," Ulysses replied. "It was meant to straighten some backbones out there. This isn't going to be easy." He turned to the boy. "Hello, Nash. I'm a little surprised to see you here."

Ulysses glanced at Uriah, a question plain on his face.

"The boy will do fine," Uriah said. "It's time he had a chance at something like this. Adventure or not, we could sure use the money."

Ulysses looked again at Nash. "I wasn't even out of short pants when I was his age," he said, more to himself than to anyone else, and then to Uriah, "I wish you well. If you have any trouble, come in. I'd rather give you the money than see either of you hurt."

"I know that, Ulysses, but we wouldn't take the money."

"I know, Uriah. I know."

The three walked back toward the big house and the barn, where the horses were being cared for, Ulysses and Uriah talking about the ditch the Brues hoped to cut the next summer, Nash thinking about Ulysses's speech.

By the time the horses were ready and the good-byes said, the group of men destined, like Uriah and Nash, for the Dry Creek camp had already gone.

"No matter, Uriah," Ulysses said. "You've been there before. Swing around that ridge there and follow it to the top. You'll cut their trail, and you can follow them into camp."

Nash was quiet as he and his father rode from the ranch, but after they reached the top of the ridge, he kicked Nell up beside his father's roan.

"Was it really like that, like Ulysses said?" he asked.

"Yes, it was like that. Ulysses polished it up a little. He's accustomed to speaking to people who don't know the West, so he doctored a little. But it's all true.

"He left a little out, too. There were a number of those 'rustlers' strung up who weren't rustlers at all, just men alone where the cattlemen didn't think they should be. It was a different world then. Times have changed."

"That man who pushed me, Dad. What were you talking to him about?"

"Just the weather, boy. Just the weather."

But Nash suspected from the edge in his father's voice that more than the weather had been discussed.

3

They came into camp four hours later.

It was a broad-bottomed coulee, leading like an arm stuck straight out from Dry Creek. The creek was frozen nearly solid from the cold, but as the Brues rode up, a man was chipping a hole in the ice for the horses. There was a stand of lodgepole pine against the rims at the head of the meadow and a scattering of cottonwoods following the low ground that carried the water from melting snowbanks through the coulee in the spring.

It was a good spot for a camp. It was sheltered for the most part from the wind, and ranch hands from the Lazy KT had cut lodgepole to build a corral against the rimrocks for the horses. Shelter for the men was another matter. The thirty or so hunters assigned to the Dry Creek camp set about making themselves as comfortable as possible. Some of the men had tents, and Nash could hear their curses as they tried to pound stakes into the frozen ground. Tents were a luxury most of the hunters could ill afford. A village based more on imagination than substance was beginning to form, and the look of the jerry-built contrivances made Nash wonder what would happen if a bad storm swept through the area.

"We've got to hurry, Nash," Uriah said. "We can't be caught out in this country without shelter." They found two small lodgepole pines standing off from the heavy stand of timber that marked the head of the coulee and the horse corral.

Uriah dismounted and tugged at the gear strapped behind the saddle. He pulled off a large piece of canvas and spread it over the snow.

"Unload the gear here," he said. "Keep it on the canvas so it won't get wet."

Nash struggled with the packs, heavy sheepskin gloves making his hands clumsy. His father walked out a small square in the snow with the two trees as corners.

"I'll take the horses over and get them water and some oats," Uriah said. "You take the saw and cut these trees off about shoulder high. Fall them back down the valley. That's where the wind will come from if it comes. Then clean all the snow out of the area I marked. All the snow. Take it down to the ground. If I'm not back by then, take the ax and start lopping off the branches. Shake all the snow off them and put them on the ground in the cleared-off area. We want the branches about a foot thick. We'll lay a tarp over that and make a mattress. You get cold from the ground up. Get with it, boy. No time for dawdling."

Nash set about his tasks as his father led off the two horses. The Swede saw cut into the soft pine easily. First Nash undercut the notch on the creek side of the tree. Then he completed the notch and felled the trees with cuts from the opposite side. Sawing warmed him considerably, and he felt good, too, about dropping the trees exactly where his father had told him to. He took out the single-bitted ax he used to cut firewood at home. The hickory handle felt easy in his hands; if not an old friend, at least a long acquaintance.

He walked up the length of the trees, lopping off boughs, being careful always to trim from the opposite side of the trunk as his father had taught him. "Cut there, and if the ax bounces off, it won't bury itself in your leg." Good advice.

He took one of the larger boughs and swept out the floor of what would be their home for the next couple of days. Just as he was finishing that, his father walked up.

"Looks good," he said. They both picked up the boughs and spread them on the floor of the lean-to. Then his father took the saw and cut both poles about fifteen feet in length. With rope, he lashed each pole to its standing butt, and then tied the remaining treetop poles across the top and bottom of the lean-to, completing the structure for the roof.

"You, Nash. Go up along those rims and start hauling down some rocks. We need some big ones to pin down the canvas."

While Uriah stretched canvas and pinned it, Nash hauled rocks. Then he helped his father carry the rest of the gear inside, storing it in the low end of the wedge. Inside it was surprisingly warm. The canvas held the air in one place long enough for the sun to warm it.

"Be sure you don't drag any snow in here. We have to keep this dry," Uriah said. "Now we need a fire, unless you aren't hungry."

It was another private joke. Nash was always hungry, or at least, that's what his father said.

Nash walked over to the stand of pines. Cowhands from the Lazy KT had cut a stack of dry pine, and hunters had already taken freely from the pile. Nash grabbed an armload and carried it back to the camp. As he started back for a second load, he heard his father splitting some of the wood into kindling. In the cold, the logs split at the touch of the ax blade, frozen moisture inside the wood making it brittle.

By the time he returned, his father had a fire going in a makeshift fireplace. The family's Dutch oven rested on a steel grill over the flames. "Nothing like Mary's stew to warm you up," his father said, and Nash nodded, feeling the warmth of the fire against his face.

The two ate with relish, and after they had mopped up the last of the stew with bread sliced from a fresh loaf from home, Nash and his father scoured the tin utensils with snow.

It was full dark and colder. Both crowded the fire, warming hands and feet. The other men had set a bonfire downhill about in the center of the little tent village, and a crowd was gathering there, one and two at a time.

Nash was watching the light play against the men below when he heard steps behind him. He turned just as the bearded man of that afternoon stepped into the circle of light thrown out by the Brue campfire.

"Well, ain't this cozy," he said. "Daddy and his little boy out camping in the hills. You better get down there, boy. There's a man there going to tell us all about the wolf. You're going to find out this is no place for kids still sucking at their mommy's teat."

Uriah came to his feet in one smooth motion, fists doubled, but the stranger moved away, laughing a nasty little laugh.

Uriah had taken one step as though to follow the bearded man when the Brue camp had another visitor. It was Jack Flynn, the association representative.

"Who is he?" Uriah asked through clenched teeth.

"Wouldn't pay too much attention to him," Flynn said. "He's got quite a reputation in Billings for beating up old men and drunks. He's been known to cuff a woman around now and then, too. But he doesn't usually tangle with anybody he doesn't outweigh by fifty or sixty pounds.

"He likes to be called Bullsnake. But he probably wouldn't like it so much if he knew that people call him that because he's all hiss and no vinegar." Flynn chuckled at his joke and then added, "You might come down. Some of the nice lads have promised to keep me in whiskey while I tell them what I know about the wolf. And I'll talk as long as the whiskey holds out. It might give you some idea of what you got into here."

"Who's the man with Bullsnake?" Uriah asked.

"Name's William Maxwell. Watch out for him. He's about half crazy, and he's handy with a knife. Bullsnake struts his stuff when Maxwell's backing him up."

They rose, threw another log on the fire, and walked down to the bonfire.

The fire cast the scene below in an eerie amber light. Light and shadows from the flames flickered through the crowd, lending movement where there was none, building strange images on a backdrop of milling men. From the crowd came the occasional glint of whiskey bottles, steel, and brass, and the muffled sound of voices that quieted as Flynn approached.

Flynn took a place on the far side of the fire, and most of the men there edged around so they could see his face as he spoke. His face was something to see. Low light from the fire put the bones in stark relief, his eyes hidden in a bank of shadow. In that light and time and space, Flynn seemed nothing more than a skull hanging between the black of the night and the yellow of the fire.

Flynn took a deep swig from a bottle that floated out to him from the depths of the crowd and began to speak.

"There are a lot of stories that men tell about this wolf. I can't tell you all of them. I can tell you only what I know, what I have seen with my own eyes, and what ol' Charley told me."

The bottle rose again to his lips.

"It all began with ol' Charley Spencer. He was a trapper. He had been a buffalo hunter once, and he never really shed himself of the stink of that. Maybe that's why he always lived alone.

"He had a cabin up here. Some of you will likely run across it. It wasn't much more than a lean-to, but it suited Charley just fine. Anyhow, Charley took hides in winter and collected bounty for coyotes and wolves during the summer. He didn't make much money, but then he didn't need much. There were plenty of deer and antelope around, and he wasn't above butchering a calf now and then for a change of diet, even if it didn't belong to him. He made enough to keep himself in flour, salt, and tobacco, and that's about all he needed.

"He was running a trapline, and one morning he set out to check it. He was coming downwind into one of the sets when he heard what he thought was a snarl. He didn't want the animal to chew off its foot before he got there, so he picked up his pace a little.

"Anyway, he came up to the clearing where the trap was, and he saw this wolf. It was a beautiful animal, white as snow with dark bands around the eyes and tapering off to gray at the tail. At first he couldn't tell how really big the animal was. It was crouching at the far end of the chain, hidden a little behind a rock. Well, as soon as Charley saw it, it had his complete attention. Those eyes. There was something about those big green eyes. Charley was staring at the wolf, kind of mesmerized when it leapt at him. All teeth and claws and eyes, like a messenger from hell, it was, and coming across that clearing on the fly. But before it got to Charley, the chain fetched up against its leg and it hit the ground with a thump.

"By then Charley knew what he was doing again, and he took his gun butt and clubbed it alongside the head, and it crumpled to the ground. Even then with it laying there in a heap, Charley knew he had something special, something no one else had ever seen before. So he rigged up a muzzle for it and tied all four feet together. Then he hitched it up to a tree so it was hanging upside down about four feet off the ground.

"Well, ol' Charley went back to his cabin and hitched up his horse to the wagon and came back where the wolf was. He had a hard time getting his horse to go anywhere near that clearing. She could smell that wolf a mile off and hear him thrashing against those ropes. If it had been anybody but Charley, the horse wouldn't have gone, but he was never a man to spare an animal. He got out his whip and worked her over something awful. It was a shame what he would do to that mare, but he finally got the rig backed underneath the wolf. He let the rope go, and the wolf hit the bed of that wagon like a boulder.

"That animal stood waist high to a tall man, and probably outweighed Charley by twenty pounds, and he was a long way from being little.

"It was an incredible animal . . . and those green eyes."

A shudder went through Flynn, and he stood there for a moment staring at something none of them could see, something he could never forget. The wolf's eyes were captivating, pulling the viewer into their depths until he felt as though he were suspended alone—oh God, how alone—in a sea of green.

He shuddered again, took a healthy swig of whiskey and continued. "That wolf was scrambling around the wagon box, trying to get up, so Charley tied its feet to the tailgate and dropped a slipknot over its head. Then he headed for Billings. Every time the wolf moved, Charley would pull that slipknot till the animal started wheezing and its eyes bugged out. I know, because I met him on the trail going in, and he was showing off a little. I told him he should kill it, that was the only thing to do. But he wouldn't have none of that. He was having too much fun, he said."

Flynn paused a moment, remembering.

"First thing he did when he got to town was to go to the blacksmith. The smithy rigged up a little cage for Charley out of some scrap wrought iron he had, and they dropped the wolf in that. It was half dead by then. Then Charley went over and collected the bounty on the coyotes and other wolves he had killed that summer and went on a spree.

"He dragged that big white wolf with him wherever he went. He kept it in the back of the wagon covered with a tarp. Everywhere Charley went a pack of dogs followed that wagon like it was a bitch in heat, yapping and growling and carrying on. And ol' Charley sat in that din and laughed and laughed and laughed.

"It was Indian summer then, and still hot down around Billings. It must have been a hundred fifty degrees under that tarp, and Charley, he never gave that wolf a drink of water or a bone to chew on. It was pitiful, and I was sorely tempted to sneak up to that cage while Charley was getting soused and put a bullet through the wolf's brain. But I really couldn't do that downtown. You never know where one of those bullets is going to go after it's done what you want it to.

"Then, too, there was Charley. He was getting crazier

by the hour. Whiskey did that to him, or maybe whiskey just brought out the craziness that was in him. He'd go into a bar and buy a drink, and then start talking about the devil wolf he had out in the wagon. That's what he called it, a 'devil wolf.' That would perk up the interest right away, and the boys would want to take a look at it.

"Then ol' Charley would say he might show them the wolf if they would buy him a round or two of drinks. Well, there was no time at all before he had more whiskey than he could ever drink. That was funny, too, because after a while, the whiskey didn't seem to matter to him. Just being around that wolf made him drunk.

"Anyway, that went on for two days, and then Charley dropped into the Stockman to start his show all over again. He was cadging drinks when this rough-looking character steps up to him. He was a trapper, and he ran dogs too. He had a few trackers and some greyhounds, but mostly he had a killer dog.

"It was a mastiff, the biggest thing I've ever seen, brindle-colored and striped like a big cat. That dog had a head on him the size of a hogshead, and it was meaner than Charley. Those greyhounds would run a coyote down and tumble it, and by the time it got back to its feet, the killer would be on it. He'd pick up the coyote and shake it like a rag doll, and it would be dead before it hit the ground.

"Well, that stranger steps up to Charley and says the wolf ain't worth a pile of buffalo chips compared to his dog, and he's willing to do more than talk and drink, he's willing to bet money on it.

"You shoulda heard the shout that went up from that

bar, but Charley wasn't so drunk that he didn't take a minute to think about it, and then he agreed."

Flynn quaffed another slug of whiskey, and then explained how they did it.

"The news spread like a prairie fire carried on a hot August wind, and an hour later, those two and two hundred more were down at the stockyard bidding pen. It has walls about twelve feet high, made out of planks with seats around the top where the cattlemen and buyers sit. It was a natural arena.

"First," Flynn continued, "the stranger leads in the killer dog, and all at once that place quiets down. That's the kind of dog he was. He stood there in the arena like he knew what was expected of him, and like he's above it somehow.

"There had already been a lot of betting, but when the crowd saw that dog, the odds changed considerable. Then they brought the wolf's cage up to the gate. The wolf was lying in the bottom, and at first, I thought he was dead. Then I saw his sides heaving a little as he tried to breathe. The crowd started getting ugly. They'd been had, they said. If they'd known what kind of shape that wolf was in they would never have bet on him at any odds.

"But when the gate opened on that cage and the wolf got up, they stopped talking. Even then, without food or water for days, even with his head hanging down like he didn't have the strength to lift it, that wolf was a magnificent animal. He stumbled into the arena and started looking around like he was calculating some way to get out of there. . . .

"The dog just stood stock still like he didn't even see

that wolf. And then, when the crowd was so quiet you could hear those two animals breathing, then the stranger leaned over the edge of the arena and said, 'Kill.' Just like he was passing the time talking about the weather, he said, 'Kill.'

"That dog headed for the wolf like there was nothing in the world he hated more. He was all teeth and muscle and bone, and he meant to kill himself a wolf.

"The wolf sidestepped the first rush kind of clumsy, like, and the dog crashed into the wall like he meant to go clear through it. Then he swung around real fast, faster than you would think a dog like that could move, and lunged again.

"The wolf was moving a little better by then. Maybe he'd worked the stiffness out of his muscles after having laid in that cage for so long, but it seemed that he was pulling strength straight from the earth like that Greek wrestler who got up good as new every time he was thrown down.

"It must have gone on for five or ten minutes: the dog trying to get hold of the wolf, pin him against the wall, and the wolf always slipping away, just kind of gliding around that ring.

"It seemed kind of funny then, because I didn't know what he was up to, but the wolf seemed more interested in the people around the ring than he was in the dog that was trying to kill him. Then he saw Charley. He kind of stopped. That was just the opening the dog had been waiting for. He hit that wolf with his shoulder and knocked him clear into the wall. He was on him in a second.

"There they were, jaw to jaw, and the men screaming. They wanted to see the kill. The money didn't matter to them then. They just wanted to see those animals tear each other to pieces.

"For a minute, it looked like the mastiff was going to do just that, but the wolf got out from under that killer dog. I don't know how he did it, but he did. And on his way up, he reached under that dog and gutted him. I'd never seen anything like that. That big old mastiff was standing there on his own guts, whining.

"The stranger was screaming for a gun, and ol' Charley was yelling that nobody was going to kill his wolf. But the stranger didn't want to kill the wolf, he wanted to kill his dog. He wanted to put that magnificent animal out of its misery.

"Something like that would never occur to ol' Charley, so they were yelling and wrestling with each other. Finally, the stranger shoved Charley, and I guess that's what saved his life."

Flynn stopped again and took another pull on the bottle. It was then that Nash felt the silence, the rapt attention of the men in the crowd. Every eye was riveted on the old Irishman. No one moved. No one drank. Flynn's eyes peered into the icy dark, seeing things his listeners could scarcely imagine. When he spoke again, it was in a whisper.

"That wolf had been waiting for Charley to get within reach, and when the scuffle took Charley to the edge of the arena, that wolf went up the wall like he was just as accustomed to running straight up as he was to running flat out. When he got up as high as he could go, he took a swipe at Charley with teeth that looked like they could split a cow's hind leg. It was just then that the stranger shoved Charley, and the wolf missed Charley's throat, but his arm was laid open to the bone. I saw it! I was standing there, and I saw the whole thing!

"By then the stranger had a rifle, and he put a bullet through the mastiff's head. Then he just walked out, and nobody ever saw him again.

"Charley was screaming for a rifle too. He had wrapped his shirt around his arm and pretty much stopped the bleeding.

"I was kind of sorry to see that wolf get killed, but I knew in the end that it would be the kindest thing. Charley told me during the fight that he had bet all his poke from the summer's bounty hunting on the dog. He figured with that wolf starved down, it wouldn't have a chance. Charley was mean even when he was feeling good, and he sure wasn't feeling good after he lost his money.

"Anyway, somebody handed him a rifle, and I expected it to end right there. I should have known better, knowing Charley like I did. He grabs the rifle and turns to the crowd. 'I'll kill the first man to touch that wolf,' he says. There was no doubt he meant it, either. He was crazy as I've ever seen him, with his eyes kind of glazed. He was out of control, carried along by his craziness like a leaf in a storm.

"And then he says, 'I'm going to kill that son-of-a-bitch myself, and it's going to take a long time in the doing. He's going to pay for losing my grubstake. He's going to hurt the way my arm hurts now.'

"Charley talked a couple cowboys there into slipping a loop around the wolf's neck and heels, to get him back in the cage. But when Charley saw him stretched out and helpless, he jumped down in the ring with a cattle prod. He started laying it on that wolf like he was the source of all the world's woes, big, deep thumps each time he hit him. Finally one of the cowboys said if Charley hit the wolf again, he'd let his end of the rope go. That quieted Charley right down. Even in the shape he was, that wolf would have cut Charley to pieces if he could have reached him.

"They got the wolf loaded back on the wagon. He was really in tough shape then. I figured the wagon ride would kill him. Charley had beat him up so bad, on top of no water or food. Charley borrowed a couple bucks from me and had Doc Borlund sew up his arm. He came out of Doc's office cussing about paying two dollars for fifteen minutes' work. Then he set off.

"Well, gents, I didn't see him for the next couple days. I still had a little business to take care of in town. Her name was Millie, if I remember right," Flynn said with a grin.

A trickle of nervous laughter pattered through the crowd, like the first drops of a summer rainstorm that moves on before it gets started.

"I was on my way out to the ranch. It had cooled off all of a sudden, and there was a touch of snow on the peaks. I figured I better get back in case we had a storm coming. But on the way, I got to thinking about Charley and the wolf. I wondered if Charley had killed him yet. The more I thought about it, the more it stuck in my craw. I didn't fancy the idea of leaving that poor, dumb animal to suffer, so I decided to ride past Charley's. If the wolf was still in the cage, I'd put a bullet in it myself.

"Well, I rode up to Charley's dugout, and right away I knew there was something wrong. The door was standing open and there was no smoke coming out of the chimney. Either one would have been all right, but both together spelled trouble, just as sure as if there was a sign on the door. I thought maybe the bite had gotten infected, and he was too sick to take care of himself. But as I walked up to the cabin, I could see ol' Charley's tracks in the skiff of snow from the night before.

"There was one set came out of the cabin nice and easy, like Charley had stepped out the front door for his morning's trip to the outhouse. But then there was another set of tracks going back into the house at a run, and another set hoofing it outside again. So I started to follow those tracks. Well, right away, I saw what was wrong. . . ."

Flynn let his listeners wait a moment.

"Out back behind the cabin was the cage, but the door was open and the wolf was gone. I almost walked past it without noticing, but something pulled me back, and then I saw them. There was another set of tracks, going up to the cage and then leaving again. I knew they weren't Charley's boots. They didn't even really look like boot tracks, more like somebody had walked out there in his stocking feet or something like that. Somebody had let the wolf out. When Charley found out about it, he got his rifle and lit out after the wolf.

"I figured he'd catch the wolf, too, as sick as it likely

was by then. But I followed Charley just to be sure. The trail led down a ridge for quite a while, and I knew that wolf was sick. Only sick animals run downhill like that. About a half mile from the cabin, the tracks led up to the edge of this little sandstone rim over the creek bottom. The wolf had walked up to the edge and slipped off. You could see where he'd bounced off the rocks on the way down, and then Charley's tracks, going down right after him.

"I wasn't as eager as ol' Charley was. There was a lot of heavy cedar down there along the creek. Sick or not, that wolf wasn't something I wanted to meet up with in cover like that, so I started to walk downstream along that rim. Well, it wasn't but a little while before I picked up their tracks down below the creek. I was going along as quiet as I could, watching for Charley or the wolf.

"It was then that I saw what had happened. The trail dipped into some really heavy juniper and then popped out into a clearing on the other side. Charley was laying there. I don't know how he did it, but he had dragged himself all the way across the clearing."

Flynn stopped, and a shudder ran through his body. He took a long pull on the bottle, and then another.

"Maybe it was just the meanness in him. I don't know what else would explain it. Anybody else would have just laid down and died, but Charley pulled himself across that clearing, dragging his guts behind him. He had stepped into the juniper, and the wolf had gutted him just as clean as he had the killer dog."

Flynn paused waiting for the murmur that ran through the crowd to die before he continued.

"When I got there, the wolf was still there, just sitting, watching. He'd been there all that time, watching Charley die. He looked up at me, and all I could see was those emerald eyes. I thought, Oh my God, I'm dead, too. But the wolf just looked at me and disappeared. He just disappeared. I went down to Charley, but he was cold by then, so I got his wagon and took him back to the cabin and buried him."

He stopped and looked into the fire for what seemed to be a long time, light and shadow playing across his face. "Ain't anybody out there got a bottle of whiskey? This one died on me," Flynn said, turning and flinging it as far as he could. "Anyhow, that's the last time I saw that beautiful beast. There's others that say they've seen his shadow going through the trees. To hear tell, everybody who has seen the wolf since then has put a mortal slug into the animal. I know that cats are supposed to have nine lives, but if all those people are telling the truth, that wolf surely puts a cat to shame.

"People say that the wolf has killed men since Charley. That could be. I don't know. A man can break a leg in this country and never be found. It's easy to blame an animal for fate. On the other hand, I can tell you that wolf took a fearsome joy in killing ol' Charley. He's killed more cattle than he could eat in a dozen lifetimes. It's the only animal I've ever seen that will kill a calf and just walk away, leaving it for the magpies.

"Some of you have asked how you'll know this wolf. But you don't have to worry about that. He lost a toe from his right front foot in Charley's trap. Some folks around here have taken to calling him Three Toes.

Others aren't nearly so charitable. He's white, like I said, with dark fur around the eyes and on the back toward the tail. There are probably other white three-toed wolves around this country, but you'll know him when you see him, the same way a greenhorn knows the rattle of a snake the first time he hears it. There's something about this wolf that touches you down deep. There's something in his eyes . . ."

Flynn broke off. A log was tossed on the fire, and a spray of sparks climbed into the cold black sky. Flynn stood at the fire like a man looking into the door of hell. He was still standing there as splinters from the group of men began to spin off into the darkness, bound for bedrolls and an uneasy sleep.

Nash and Uriah walked back to their camp in silence. They tossed a couple chunks of wood on the embers of the fire and crawled into the lean-to.

It was warmer there, but not much, and both hurried to shed their outer clothes and climb into their bedrolls. They said good night and rolled over to go to sleep, but Nash couldn't take his mind off the wolf. In his mind's eye, he could see him, head down, poised like a snake to strike, long white fangs and green eyes. Eyes as green as the swimming hole on the creek back home. Nash lay rigid, pretending to sleep. He lay there for what seemed to be hours, and he was still awake when his father muttered, "What the hell have I gotten us into?"

4

The lean-to the next morning made all those cold mornings back home at the cabin seem tropical in comparison. A thick rime of frost lined the inside of the canvas, and when Nash reached up and touched it, it dusted down onto his neck. Nash didn't want to leave the relative warmth of his bedroll, but he knew he must. It was still dark and the light of the kerosene lanterns bobbed around the campground. Nash dressed and crawled outside to the sound of muttered voices and the rattle of saddles and bridles being put to horses. Uriah had already fried some sidepork, and Nash fell to, sopping up some of the grease with bread sliced from one of his mother's fresh loaves. Uriah had eaten and was sipping coffee made with water taken from the creek that morning.

While Nash was eating, his father walked over to the corral. When he returned, he was leading Nell and the roan. Both were saddled and ready to go.

As Nash scrubbed out the frying pan with snow, Uriah squatted down next to him. Uriah watched a few moments and then said, "You know we don't have to do this. I've been thinking about what Flynn said last night, and it might just be better if we packed up and went home. There's no shame in that. From the look of things, there's more than one party here that plans to do just that."

Nash had noticed. Men were packing up, readying themselves for the trip back to their homes. In the shade of Flynn's speech, the hunt had lost its aura. Although none of the hunters would have admitted it, Flynn had frightened them. They wanted no part of this wolf. The cattlemen could do their own killing.

Nash was wavering. He didn't like the idea of going home, admitting to the Anderson children, admitting to Ettie, to himself, that he was still more child than man. But he didn't want to track that killer wolf through these hills, either.

Just then Bullsnake stepped up behind Uriah. "Tough decision isn't it, sonny? Maybe you better ride back home on that plow horse and ask your ma. Is that what you're going to do, boy?"

Uriah stood and turned around. "I don't remember inviting you over here," he said, "and now I'm asking you to leave."

"Well, as long as you're asking, I might," Bullsnake said. "I get all upset when people aren't polite to me. I don't think you would like it much if I got upset, mister."

"I don't like you much either way," Uriah said, an edge poking out of his voice like a rock breaking the smooth flow of a stream.

Bullsnake sprang back in mock fear. "My, my, my. Pa is getting a little feisty. I better run back to my camp before I get so scared I pee my pants."

Nash saw the muscles knot along his father's shoulders, and his eyes seemed to glaze for a moment, becoming opaque. Nash had only seen that happen once before. His father had been shoeing Nell, but the big animal kept pulling away from him. Each time he positioned the shoe on the mare's hoof, she would take it away from him. He had worked on her for nearly an hour, quietly, soundlessly. Then he began muttering. It was then that Uriah's eyes turned opaque. He was holding the tiny shoeing hammer in his hands, and that was all that saved Nell's life. If Uriah had had something heavier, he would have killed her. But he didn't. He began beating her with the hammer. Nash watched, and then he had begun screaming at his father to stop. He picked up a stick and jabbed Uriah in the leg, and his father had turned, hammer upraised, and Nash thought the monster was going to strike him, kill him. Then, as Nash watched, the monster died, and his father returned. Uriah had walked rubber-legged over to a stool. He sat there shaking, pale, as though he were very ill.

Then Uriah had stared at Nash as though he were sitting naked before his son, and his eyes filled with tears. "I'm sorry. I didn't mean to do that. We'll take Nell over to the Andersons' tomorrow. He's a better farrier than I am. I'm sorry, Nash. I'm sorry."

And now Nash stood there in front of the fire and hoped that monster wouldn't come back again. He hoped he wouldn't ever see him again.

But Uriah's eyes cleared, and Bullsnake moved off, chuckling to himself.

Uriah climbed into the saddle, and Nash mounted Nell. They rode outside the circle of light from the campfires and waited a moment for their eyes to adjust to the darkness before moving on.

As they waited there, Nash asked, "What makes him mean like that?"

"I don't know, son," Uriah said. "All I know is that he

is what he is. We have enough to do worrying about what we are."

They climbed a ridge to a high, flat plateau that stretched off to the southwest for miles, and put the North Star over their right shoulders. The night was still black and the stars bright against it. Patches of grass and brush loomed out of the snow, and Nash saw a dozen wolves crouching beside the trail—until proximity transformed them into juniper and sage.

The snow muffled the sound of the horses' hooves, and as false dawn touched the sky to the east and dimmed the stark black and white relief of the night, the animals seemed almost to be swimming in a sea of white. An hour had lapsed before Uriah spoke. "There's a big coulee up here that comes off the east fork of Dry Creek. It's heavy with brush and cover. I'm going to let you off at the mouth. I want you to wait there about forty-five minutes or an hour, while I take the two horses up to the head. Then you come up along the bottom. Whenever you come to a branch bear to the right. I'll be waiting up at the top for anything you spook ahead of you.

"And Nash, I want you to be real careful. I don't think that wolf is as dangerous as Flynn said—if I did, I wouldn't let you go. But I don't want you taking any chances anyway. Anywhere that brush gets too heavy for you to see into it, you climb the canyon wall. Just sit down and watch. Animals are funny. They'll lay real quiet while you're busting through the brush, but stop a minute, and they think you spotted them. Their nerve breaks, and that can be fatal. Remember that."

When they reached the coulee, Uriah climbed down

off his roan. He reached into his saddlebag and pulled out five twelve-gauge shells. Then, very carefully, so the sound would not alert any animals in the area, he broke open the gun's action, dropped two cartridges into the breech, and closed it.

He leaned over and whispered in Nash's ear, "You be damn careful. If a storm moves in, you climb back up the side of the coulee. I'll come down and pick you up. I'll come to you. Don't you try to find me. Take it easy. Go slow."

Nash stood in the snow listening as the sounds of the horses' hooves disappeared in the dull light. He had never felt so alone, so utterly alone. He stood there for some time, attuning his senses to the space around him. He knew he should sit down so he wouldn't stand out against the skyline when the sun rose, but he couldn't bring himself to do it. He stood there listening, poised as though for flight. He was still standing there motionless as the sun cracked the sky to the east. There was no warmth in its rays, but Nash's soul soared with the light. The wolf was a creature of the night, of bad dreams. His time was past, and Nash's beginning.

Nash slipped over the edge of the coulee and made his way down the steep hill. The coulee bottom was still in shadow, but he could easily see the other side. There were broken rims on each side carved from the sandstone slab that underlay most of the region. The slopes on both sides were steep, punctuated by pine and juniper mixed with the more common sagebrush and yucca. A sharp break at the bottom marked the course of the spring snowmelt. In some places that cut was ten feet deep or more, and it wound back and forth across the floor of the coulee like a snake. Occasionally, the coulee opened into wide meadows of five to ten acres. Elsewhere precipitous walls plunged into the cut at the bottom.

Nash knew he would have to stay close to the bottom—a den could easily be hidden in the walls—yet far enough up the slope to view what lay ahead and behind.

The fear that had fled ahead of the morning light was waiting in the shadows ahead. Nash could feel it there, a palpable presence undeterred by the weight of the twelve-gauge in his arms. As he stepped ahead, Nash could feel his heartbeat, hear the whisper of blood coursing through his arteries. He wondered if the wolf could hear it too. He wondered if the wolf were waiting, lying under one of the juniper bushes ahead, listening to the heartbeat of his approaching prey, savoring the prospect of stilling that heart and leaving the prairie quiet again.

Nash stalked on. Hunting deer with his father, he spent much of his time watching the ground, taking care that he didn't snap a twig or dislodge a stone and send a deer rattling out of sight to safety. But it was different now. Nash felt an even greater need for quiet. Maybe if he could slip through that coulee in near perfect silence, with no more sound than that of the stretching of his sinews, the wolf wouldn't hear him. Maybe the wolf would sleep on, oblivious of the boy gliding past on soundless feet.

Nash had never seen a coulee as he saw this—not as a

hunter, but as prey. Each bush, each rock, tree, and cut might have hidden the wolf. Nash's eyes scoured the landscape looking for the slightest clue; a trail through the snow leading into a bush and not continuing out the other side, the hint of a predator's hot breath against the frosty air. Anything and everything that might give him the split-second warning it would take to swing the shotgun's muzzle on line, to cock the ornate curved hammers that rode along each side of the Damascus barrel.

He had walked along less than a quarter of a mile, step by hesitating step, when he came to it. The coulee had narrowed, and he had been forced to scramble along the sidehill. That slowed his pace even more. He kicked the soles of his boots into the hillside for purchase, sacrificing silence for safety. Still each step threatened to send him plunging to the bottom. The coulee took a sharp bend to the east, and as he edged around the hill, he saw it.

It was just as Uriah had said. The coulee opened into a little park, but it was wall-to-wall juniper and pine. The brush was so thick there was no hope of seeing into it or walking quietly through it.

Nash paused for a moment, looking below. A whole pack of bloodthirsty wolves could lie in ambush there, waiting for an unwary deer—or man—to stumble into the brush. Nash stood there, and the fear grew in him, gnawing at his gut like a live animal.

Then he realized the pain wasn't imaginary but real. Oh, hell, he thought, gas.

Nash knew he couldn't wait. Not long anyway. He and his large intestine had worked out a bargain long ago.

The large intestine wouldn't bother him until it was absolutely necessary. Sometimes two or three days stretched between those times. But when the call came, Nash was expected to answer with very little hesitation.

The bargain had been necessary, the result of the gap-sided, splinter-ridden, one-holer out back behind the Brue cabin. It was a miserable place. In winter the thought of sitting down on that seat with a wind whipping a miniblizzard through the walls was enough to give anyone pause. And still winter was better than summer. In summer the stench was unbearable. Lime dumped down the hole occasionally would help, but only for a while. Sometimes at night the reek of putrification would drift down toward the house and send everyone outside to evening chores. Nobody lingered at the outhouse, even if the Sears Roebuck catalogue was there for reading—and other purposes, too. Flies buzzed around the building in a cloud, and sometimes Nash thought he would inhale one of the creatures. Knowing as he did what drew the flies to the outhouse, the thought of one of them touching him was enough to make him gag. It was because of that one-holer that the bargain had been struck. And now he had no time to waste.

Nash searched the hillside frantically for a ledge or rock, any place level enough he could squat there without sliding or tumbling down the hill. There was none. Nash had no choice. His need overcame his fear. He would go into the brush. There was a smooth log there. He would make his way to that.

Nash slipped, scrambled, and slid down the hill. He didn't care about noise then. He hoped that the sound would frighten anything hidden below out of the brush before he got there. But if it didn't, that was all right too. If the wolf, that awesome, fear-inspiring beast, had stepped out of the brush to greet him fang and claw, Nash wouldn't have given him so much as a fare-thee-well. Nash had more important things on his mind.

Branches tugged at Nash's clothes, as he headed into the brush at a run. He had to reach that log. He did, just in time. He jerked down his pants, and fumbled for a minute at the flap buttons on his long johns. Then he sat down.

Oh, blessed relief—but not for long.

The wolf popped into his mind again, and the image was worse than ever. Nash was about as vulnerable as anyone could be. The wolf could take Nash now before he could even raise the shotgun leaning beside him on the log. Wouldn't that be something? It was one thing to be killed by a wolf like the one they were hunting. There was more than a little romance in that. He'd be like ol' Charley Spencer, and when men gathered at night around campfires, stories would be told about him and the killer wolf.

But what if the wolf got him while he was sitting bare-bottomed over a log, taking a crap? There wasn't much romance in that. The vision was clear in his mind's eye, and it wasn't pleasant. His father riding stern-faced into the homestead, leading old Nell burdened with an empty saddle. His mother frantic for word of her son. Uriah climbing down from the roan: "I'm sorry, Mary. But I've got bad news. Nash didn't make it. The wolf got him. He was sitting there on a log, defecating (he would use the word *defecating* so as not to offend Mary), and the wolf sneaked up behind him and grabbed him. There was nothing he could do, what with his pants down around his knees. He tried to get up, but the pants dumped him right there in the snow."

And then his father would laugh. He wouldn't be able to help it, any more than August in Montana could help being hot or January cold. He would be truly sorry about Nash going and all, but he would laugh just the same. And Nash bet his mother would laugh too. He'd be dead, and they'd be sitting around laughing at the predicament he'd been in. And what about Ettie? She would tell everybody at school. Probably when she was married and had kids of her own, she would think of Nash Brue and the way he died and laugh up a storm.

It just wasn't fair, the way he was going to be treated if the wolf jumped him now. Nash was getting a little mad. He was beginning to hope that wolf would come. Nash would show him a thing or two.

Then it occurred to Nash how ridiculous the situation was, and he began to laugh at himself, his chuckles trickling into a flood of guffaws. He laughed till tears came to his eyes. He wasn't as afraid of the wolf anymore. Somehow the laughter had eased the fear. He wiped himself with the wad of paper he had carried in his pocket and stood, hitching up his pants. Bring on the wolf. Nash was ready.

He settled into an easy hunting rhythm, slipping through the coulee, moving quietly from cover to cover, pausing and watching for some moments before padding along. He had noticed the tracks some time ago, rambling across the hillside on the opposite side. He didn't know for sure what had left that sign in the snow. The trail meandered like a deer searching here and there for browse. But it could just as well have been a wolf. Nash really didn't want to know. He didn't want to walk across the coulee to look. He just wanted to keep the tracks on the far side. The coulee was narrowing, and Nash was forced to walk higher and higher on the hillside to keep his footing on the precipitous walls. He was walking along just below the crest when his father called to him from only a few feet away.

"Glad to see the wolf didn't eat you, boy. Would have had a hard time explaining that to your mother. Get a bite to eat out of the saddlebag, then come over and help me load up a deer. She was moving ahead of you. We'll eat well this trip."

Nash took a loaf of bread from the saddlebags, cut two slices, and slipped a slab of roast venison between them and sat down to eat. Meanwhile, Uriah opened a can of peaches and squatted down next to Nash. Each took turns stabbing the peach halves with his knife. When the fruit was gone, they split the juice, drinking from the can. Canned peaches were a treat, and Nash savored his. When they were done, Uriah tossed the can down into the coulee.

"Give me a hand with the doe, Nash."

The deer was fat and in fine shape. She had not yet lost her reserve from summer, and a thick layer of white suet lay heavy along her spine.

Uriah and Nash quartered the animal, taking only the hindquarters and the tender steaks that lay along the back. The heart and the liver were dropped into a sack and tied, together with the meat, on Nell behind Nash's saddle. Had they been nearer home, they would have taken all the deer, loading her into a wagon and carrying her home to hang until she aged. Then they would have processed the meat. But they weren't home. When they were done, both scrubbed the blood off their hands in the snow.

"Time to go, boy. It'll be near dark by the time we get to camp."

Uriah and Nash mounted and nudged their horses into a walk. On the way, Nash told his father about the coulee, about the tracks he had seen. He did not tell his father about the incident in the brush.

Uriah had spent most of the day carving himself into the landscape, trying to disappear into the bush where he was hiding. Only his eyes moved as they searched the landscape for some sign of the wolf. When he breathed, he let the air go so slowly the vapor was not visible. He had been sitting for more than an hour, wriggling his toes to keep the blood flowing through them.

He watched only the upwind course of the coulee. Nothing would be wandering across the plateau to his back. It was too open, too exposed, too dangerous. Besides, any animal downwind would catch his scent and avoid the ambush.

He had been watching the deer for some time. She was meandering slowly, stopping to browse on sage and buck brush poking through the snow. He might not have shot her, but she continued to walk ingenuously toward the bush where he was hidden. It was inevitable that she would catch his scent on the breezes playing through the coulee, and when she did, she would spook. And that would spook any other animals in the vicinity. So he shot her. The slug broke her shoulder, coursed through her lungs and lodged under the rib cage on the other side. She fell immediately, struggling quietly in the snow while the life leaked out of her. Uriah didn't watch. Instead his eyes searched the walls of the coulee, looking for animals that might have been frightened into flight by the crack of the rifle. But there were none, so Uriah walked over to the stricken doe. She kicked just a little as he cut her throat.

"It was a good thing it took you so long to come up that coulee, Nash," Uriah said.

Nash looked quizzically at his father.

"Well, I was thinking," Uriah said. "I was eating a piece of jerky and thinking about how cold it is today, and all at once it came to me. The only thing wrong with our plans so far is that I get cold. You do a great job of stumbling around in the brush and chasing the game up to me. That doe was so interested in the racket you were making that she didn't even notice me, but I was a little uncomfortable sitting up here waiting for you.

"I know your daddy's comfort is of the utmost importance to you, so I sat here trying to figure out how we could best take advantage of your brush-bucking ability and my penchant for sitting.

"I think I've got it worked out. Maybe tomorrow I'll just stay in camp by the fire and send you out to chase the wolf back to me. That way I won't get cold. What do you think of that?"

Nash worked hard to nip the grin that was trying to take root in his face. "Well, Dad, I think that's a good idea," he said. "But I hate the idea of you sitting out in the cold with just a fire to keep you warm. Maybe you should just stay in bed and leave the flap to the lean-to untied. I could drive the wolf in to you, and you could run your socks under his nose until he passed out."

"I like your thinking, boy, but maybe I should carry a stick, just in case the socks don't work."

"I've been in the lean-to at night," Nash retorted. "The socks will do just fine."

Uriah whooped, and the two rode away from the coulee with the sound of their laughter surrounding them. It was still light when they dropped off the ridge into the campsite on Dry Creek, but for a moment Nash thought they had come to the wrong place.

The night before the camp had been full. This afternoon it looked like a gold camp after the color ran out. Bullsnake and Maxwell were still there with Flynn and three or four others, but fully half the camp had gone. Then, as though to fill the vacuum left by the others, there was a newcomer. He was sitting on a log at the edge of the camp, huddled in a dark blanket.

Flynn walked up as the two reined in their horses near their lean-to. "Glad to see you back. Getting a little lonesome. I was beginning to think I'd only have Maxwell and old Hiss and Vinegar for company."

"What happened to the crowd?" Uriah asked.

"Oh, that was a sad thing," Flynn replied. "Some of them had a bad feeling during the night that something was wrong on the old homestead. Some of them thought their horses were looking a little sickly. Some of them said they didn't like the idea of killing the wolf anyway. But I figure that most of them were just a little scared." Flynn stopped for a moment, eyeing the meat tied behind Nash's saddle. "I've got about half a bottle of whiskey left. I'd be happy to sacrifice some of that nectar for a couple of those loin steaks."

"No need for the whiskey," Uriah said. "I was going to spread the steaks around a little anyway. You're welcome to what you can eat. Come on back in an hour or so, and we'll fry some up."

Flynn grinned his thanks and walked off toward his tent.

Nash and Uriah busied themselves, unloading the meat. They put the haunches in a double burlap sack and hung it from a nearby tree. The sack would keep magpies out of the meat, and it hung high enough to discourage whatever scavengers might come into camp.

"I'll bed the horses," Uriah said. "You might go down and get some water. Ask the newcomer if he wants some meat. Maxwell and Bullsnake can come over here and ask if they want some."

Nash grabbed some kindling and a page from the Sears Roebuck catalogue and started a fire on last night's ashes. The wood was dry and burst into flame. Nash added larger and larger sticks, building a bed of coals for cooking later. Then he picked up the big blue enameled coffeepot by the bail and began walking toward the creek. He had taken only a few steps when he hesitated and changed directions, moving toward the man wrapped and invisible in the dark blanket.

Nash approached the figure with more than a little trepidation. He was at that awkward age between childhood and adulthood. He didn't yet feel easy in the company of strangers, and given the chance, he would have preferred hanging back and letting his father do the talking. That hesitancy increased as he neared the stranger. The blanket was not a blanket but a buffalo robe. Nash had seen enough of them draped over furniture at the Jeffries home to recognize that. The robe hung over the man's head like a hood, only the tips of his feet were showing, and those feet were clad not in boots but in moccasins. Indian! The man, if it did indeed prove to be a man, was an Indian.

5

It wasn't that Nash had not seen Indians before. He had, most of them scattered like debris around the rowdier saloons in Billings. In daylight they hid in their trade blankets and at night in alcohol. They were always there, blanket recriminations, ashes of a people.

And there was that time at the homestead. It was summer, and Nash was too young yet to work in the fields. He had done his morning chores and was spending his free time until evening chores "underfoot," as his mother said. Bored with the events unfolding in the kitchen, Nash had stepped out onto the porch—and there they were. Two families wrapped in rags, borne by a wagon. They sat there silently, the patience of ages on their faces, and then Mary was standing behind him, her hands on his shoulders. Nobody moved. Each was waiting for a cue from the other. Finally, the oldest Indian stood in the wagon and pointed to his belly. "Food," he said, his hand moving in an arc encircling those quiet staring faces behind him. Nash was fascinated. A wagonload of people, men, women, and children, and not a flicker of life or hope. Only stoicism. Nash's attention was so focused on those faces that he didn't hear the horse's hooves at first. It wasn't until the faces on the wagon turned toward the sound that Nash really heard the clatter of hooves.

It was a scene he would never forget. His father, working in the field by the creek, had stripped the harness off Nell, and he was riding her bareback, a coil of harness lines in one hand. Nell was spectacular. She careened into the yard, her hooves picking up saucers of mud and spraying them behind her. Uriah's hat had blown off. The wind had pulled his hair back from his face, all bone and sinew in its intensity.

Just as it looked as though Nell would run into the Indians' wagon, Uriah pulled back on the reins and the big horse sat down on her haunches. Uriah leapt off her back and hit the ground running. He reached the step in two bounds and swept Mary and Nash off their feet, one on each arm, as though they were nothing more than sheaves of wheat. He carried them inside, kicking the door shut with his feet. He put them down and reached for the shotgun inside the door.

Mary shouted, "No!"

But Uriah seemed not to hear. He broke open the gun and jammed two shells into the chambers. Then he opened the door and stepped out on the porch. Nash stood behind his father, almost in a state of shock. But stunned as he was, he noticed the tremor in his father's hands as the bore of the twelve-gauge swept up to encompass the people in the wagon.

"Git!" Uriah shouted. "Git, or so help me God, I'll kill you all."

Nash heard the ugly *snick* as Uriah cocked the two hammers on the shotgun. The old Indian dropped to his seat and wheeled the wagon out of the yard. And through it all, there hadn't been a flicker of emotion on the faces of those others in the wagon. It was as though life and death held neither promise nor threat to them.

Uriah stood there on the porch long after the wagon had disappeared, and then Mary stepped up behind him. "You have to let it go, Uriah. You have to let it go."

And Uriah's reply, wrenched out of his gut, "I can't, Mary. I can never forget."

Nash didn't understand what happened that day. Neither his mother nor his father had spoken of it since. But he knew that his father had been afraid for Nash and his mother. And from that time on Nash knew, deep in his mind where nightmares dwell, that Indians were different and dangerous. The memory of that day was fresh in his mind as Nash forced himself to walk up to the figure crouched on the log.

"My dad said I should ask you if you wanted some meat," Nash said. "Do you?"

The man shifted, and Nash found himself staring into a tunnel made by the hood over the stranger's face. Deep down in the darkness there, Nash saw the glint of light reflected from the man's eyes, like starlight bouncing off a black pool at night. Still the stranger said nothing.

"Well, uh, I've got to get some water now," Nash said, and he fled toward the creek.

He filled the coffeepot through a hole chopped in the ice that lay in a rough sheet over the stream. And all the time he watched the icy water swirl into the pot, he was thinking about the trip back to the lean-to. If he walked any way but the way he had come, he would be showing the fear that he felt. But if he went back by the same path, he would walk past the Indian.

Nash shivered—and not with the cold—as he walked back toward the lean-to. He kept his head down, watching his feet as he neared the stranger. He didn't want to look at the man. He didn't want to meet those eyes again. He ignored the call the first time, but the second time it was more insistent. "Boy!"

Nash looked up. The man had slipped the robe off his head. He was Indian all right, but old, old past being a threat. His hair was white and sparse and combed back into two braids. His face was wrinkled as the bark of a cottonwood tree and dark as Nash's boots. The eyes were still dark pools glinting light, but Nash could see they held no malice.

"Boy, I would have some of the meat you offered."

Suddenly, Nash wasn't frightened anymore. Instead, he was intrigued. He had listened enthralled as old-timers told about their brushes with "injuns." Even at this late date, more than a decade into the twentieth century, cattlemen complained about Indians sneaking stock from ranches adjoining the reservations and then demanding a tariff before returning them to their owners.

More than a few cattle disappeared into reservation cooking pots, too, without the benefit of a bill of sale.

"Boy," the old man's breathy voice broke again into Nash's reverie. "My teeth are not so hard as they once were. Bring me soft meat."

"We have liver," Nash said. The old man nodded.

Nash walked back to the lean-to with the trace of a skip in his step. It was a lucky day. He had talked to an Indian and gotten rid of some of that damn liver at the same time. Damn liver. People who palaver with Indians can spice up their speech a little—at least, if it isn't said out loud.

Uriah was standing over by Flynn's tent talking to the Irishman. Nash threw a couple more sticks of wood on the fire and sliced off a generous chunk of the liver. Nash had detested liver for as long as he could remember, and he ate the foul stuff only at his mother's insistence. He added a little more to the old man's share and carried it back to the newcomer's fire.

"We've got more if you want it," Nash said.

The old man grunted, and as he reached toward Nash for the meat, a knife appeared from under the robe. Nash involuntarily stepped back. The knife wasn't a challenge, just an eating utensil. But the old man had been holding it under his robe, waiting. Old or not, this man wasn't to be taken for granted.

The old man sliced a strip of meat from the cooled liver and started to raise it to his lips. Then he glanced at Nash, noting the boy's barely concealed distaste. The deeply eroded rock that was the old man's face softened with what might have been a grin. "Get me that willow, boy."

Nash snipped off the willow wand where it broke through the snow and handed it to the old man, who, in turn, impaled a piece of liver on the stick and began roasting the meat over the fire. Cooking didn't take long. When the fire had painted the liver a light gray, the old man lifted it from the flame and popped it into his mouth. Nash knew the liver was still raw. The old man was aware of that. He chewed with great relish, watching the boy's face.

Nash broke the silence. "I better be going now."

But the old man stopped him. "What are you called, boy?"

"Nash. That's short for Nashua, but only my mother calls me that. What's your name?"

"Oh, I have many names. When I was a boy, they called me Gopher, because I was always poking my nose into one thing or another. Then when I became a man, I was given another name. After I stole many horses from the Blackfeet, the people called me Rides Plenty. And now the traders at the post in Lame Deer have given me yet another name. I went in there one day and did not know that the skinny trader, who has so many hairs in his nose, was watching me. He stopped me on the way out and took the things I had hidden in my shirt. He was the first to call me by my new name, Light-fingered Old Buck. That is a strong name. The traders are afraid of me now. Every time I go to the post, they say, 'Watch out, here comes that Light-fingered Old Buck.'"

A wheezing gasp that apparently passed for a chuckle shook the old man's frame. "But you can call me Grandfather."

Grandfather sliced off another piece of liver, not bothering to pass it over the flames before popping it into his mouth. "You come back after you have eaten, Nash, and I will tell you a story."

The old man studied Nash's face for a long moment, and then, apparently satisfied with what he saw, turned back to the fire.

Just then Uriah's voice floated up from below.

"Nash. Time to eat."

Uriah had sliced the loin into what he called butterfly steaks, and was in the process of coating them liberally with flour, salt, and pepper, when Nash walked into camp.

"What took you so long?" Uriah asked with an odd edge to his voice. "That water will be a long time making coffee now."

Nash poured out about half the water and set the pot and the can of coffee in front of his father. Uriah was not fussy about most things, but the making of coffee was a serious matter, not something to be entrusted to anyone who didn't drink the stuff.

Uriah had the coffeepot and the big cast-iron skillet heating over the fire by the time Flynn arrived.

"Ah, look at those steaks, will you," Flynn said, rubbing his hands together. "Fresh meat for a hot meal in a cold camp. Can't ask for much more than that."

Uriah took out three pieces of sidepork and threw them in the flying pan. When the pork began to sizzle, he sprinkled salt and pepper over it, turning the meat until it was cooked crisp. He took a piece of the sidepork and gave Flynn and Nash the last two, leaving enough grease in the frying pan for the steaks.

The smell of venison cooking began to fill the air, and all three stood watching the frying pan. After the steaks were well done, really well done—venison simply isn't eaten rare—they sat down to eat. Uriah took another loaf of Mary's bread out of the food sack, and they each tore off chunks and dipped them in the grease still left in the frying pan. They ate with a hunger only a day out in the cold could engender, and they spoke very little.

The coffee wasn't ready when the three had finished eating, but Uriah was somewhat mollified when Flynn hauled out a bottle of bourbon. Each man took a swig and sat for a moment, feeling the alcohol burn into his stomach, giving him the illusion of warmth, if not more.

Finally, Uriah spoke. "Who is he?" he asked, nodding toward the old Indian still sitting alone at his fire.

"Don't know," Flynn said. "Never saw him before. Came in sometime after you left. He doesn't have a horse, so I guess he walked here. But I don't have any idea where he was heading or why he stopped here."

"I'll tell you how he got here." Nash and Uriah both jumped a little at the bark of the gruff voice behind them. "The son-of-a-bitch smelled food and came a-begging. It always amazes me how those bastards can smell food. The way they stink, you wouldn't think they would be able to smell anything but themselves."

Bullsnake's voice was rising now. He was almost shouting, to be sure the old man could hear him. "Whoeee. If the wind don't change, the smell of that old buck is going to drive us all out of camp. It's an awful thing when a white man has to live around his kind. Ain't

83

that right, boy?" Bullsnake clapped a hand on Nash's shoulder and squeezed too hard for a friendly gesture. "Well, I gotta be going now, gents," he said, stretching out the "gents" until it seemed to be a nasty word.

When Bullsnake called over his shoulder, "Be seeing you, boy," there was just the hint of a threat in it; then he crunched away through the snow, trailing a plume of fogged air behind him.

"They see anything today?" Uriah asked.

"Hard to say," Flynn replied. "They didn't leave camp, and I sure didn't see anything around here worth shooting—nothing wild, anyway. They sat around playing gin rummy a penny a point. Wanted me to sit in, but they're a little more liberal with the rules than I like. Don't know what they're up to, but you can bet it isn't any good."

The coffee was ready, and Uriah poured a cup for Flynn and one for himself, and the two began talking about how the country was going to hell in a hand basket.

Nash interrupted. "Dad, I'm going to go up and talk to the old man for a while."

Uriah stopped talking. Nash watched the cords knot in his father's neck, and then Uriah's voice came low and hard and cold. "You can go, boy. But make sure that he understands that I'm watching him. You tell him I never hesitate taking a hoe to a rattler. You tell him that, Nash."

Nash knew the vehemence in his father's voice was not directed at him. Still, the sound of it sent shivers down his spine.

Flynn seemed not to have heard Uriah. He appeared to

be utterly fascinated by his fingernails, studying them as an artist studies a canvas.

It was cold as Nash walked away from the campfire, but he felt a chill that had nothing to do with the weather. As he neared the old man's fire, he wondered again whether he should be there, whether it would not have been better for him to stay with Flynn and his father.

As Nash came up, the old man was staring into the flames, lost in the memories he saw flickering there. Nash stood for a long moment, then brushed the snow off a rock on the other side of the fire and sat down. Still the figure in the buffalo robe was silent. Finally, just as Nash was about to leave, the old man spoke. "Do you not smell the stink in the air?"

"No," Nash said. "I don't smell anything."

"I smell something," the old man said. "It comes faintly on the wind as though from a far place, but I know it. I have smelled it many times."

"What is it?" Nash asked.

"Fear," the old man said. "I smell fear."

"You shouldn't be afraid. Bullsnake is all talk. Dad told me," Nash said, meaning to reassure the old man. But as he spoke he realized he was only reassuring himself.

The old man pulled his attention from the fire and laid it on Nash. "I am not afraid. I have not been afraid since I was a boy about your age. I smell fear on others. It burns in my nose and wrinkles the skin of the back of my neck. Fear is contagious, and as deadly as the white man's smallpox. But fear does not touch me."

At that moment fear touched Nash. There was something strange about the old man, and Nash felt as though the whisper of something unseen had flitted through the camp when the Indian spoke.

"I will tell you why I am no longer afraid. When I was a boy," the old man said in a brittle, reedy voice, "my father purified me in the sweat lodge and bathed me in the smoke of sage and took me to a secret place in the mountains where I was to await my spirit helper. We built a small shelter of brush and prayed and did as my father had been instructed to do by his father. And when all was complete, he left me there to await my vision.

"I held my arms up as though to embrace the sun. I opened myself to everything around me and watched the sun as it made its way across the heavens to its home in the west. And I rose before the sun the next morning, too, and greeted it with prayers on my lips and hope in my heart. I stood all day with no food or water, praying that the maheo would send a vision to me. I lay awake that night, my arms aching and my belly crying out for food, but my mind wanted a vision above all else. It is very important to have a vision.

"The third day was bad. My throat was so dry that I croaked when I tried to sing. My lips cracked and bled. But then I became one with the earth, with life. A deer walked by my camp and was not afraid of me. I had become part of him, and he had become part of me. I felt his life before I saw him. I felt the sun across his back and the taste of sage in his mouth, and he felt my pain. When the deer disappeared, bouncing away on stiff legs, I felt what had frightened him.

"There was a man coming toward me from the trail

86

below. I could not see or hear him, but I knew he was there. I heard him in the protest of the grass as he passed over it. And then I saw him. He was a strong man, graceful and handsome, with eyes as black and deep as a mountain lake in the moonlight. He motioned for me to follow him, and I did so without question. After we walked for a while, we began to run, gliding through the trees and across meadows ever faster, until I could see only a blur of green and blue and brown—and his back. I was running faster than I had ever run before or since. I felt I could fly, and perhaps I was flying. Had he willed it, I would have followed him into the heart of the sun, and perhaps I did.

"He slowed, and we came to a stop on a meadow that stretched to the end of the world. We were higher in the mountains than the trees grow, and every step we took was on thousands of tiny flowers, but so light was our tread that we did not crush even one. It was then that I saw the lodge. It stretched nearly to the clouds and painted on its walls was the Cheyenne circle of life. The ancient one nodded, gazing deeply into the embers of his fire.

"He held the flap and I stepped inside. In the middle of the lodge was a huge bonfire, built not of logs but whole trees, and still flames from that fire lit only the center of the lodge. The walls lay hidden in shadow. Had I not seen the lodge from the outside, had I not known it was day, I would have thought that I was sitting outside on a mountain meadow in darkest night.

"Surrounding the fire were more men than there were in all of our band. They were dressed so finely, they would have put any of my people to shame. And then, as I watched, these men turned into animals. It was then that I knew I was in the lodge of the spirit people. Buffalo was there, and Bear, and Coyote . . . all the spirit animals. I turned to look at the man who had brought me there. He was gone. Standing in his place was a wolf, but a wolf unlike any other. Wolf Spirit was handsome as a man, but as a wolf, he was beautiful. He was mostly white with dark hair around the eyes and back toward his tail. He looked almost as though he were wearing a mask. His eyes, black as a moonlit mountain lake when he was a man, had turned green, like the lake at dawn when the light from the sun strikes the water and lights its depths. I couldn't help looking into his eyes. They were as deep as forever. I could see all things that had been and all things that were yet to be.

"Then all the animals turned back into men, and Wolf Spirit said that he was to be my spirit helper, and he told me that I was to go hunting when I returned to the village and walk two days west from the camp until I came to a stream, and climb into the crook of a tree there. I was to wait there until a wolf came to me, and I was to kill it, thanking it for the gift of its life. I was to take the wolf's claws and fangs and carry them in my medicine bag. I was to skin the wolf and tan the hide myself. It was not to be touched by the hand of any other person. And when I went into battle, I was to wear the skin of that wolf over my head and down my back. Wolf Spirit told me that as long as I wore the wolfskin and carried my medicine bag I could never be killed in battle.

"Then the lodge and everything in it began spinning

like eddies along the Yellowstone. Everything disappeared. I awoke to find myself lying on the ground outside the brush lodge where my father had left me.

"I was tired and weak, but I drank from a nearby stream and walked back to the village. My father had been watching, and he met me before I reached the lodges. He walked ahead of me into camp, singing, 'Behold my son, he has had a great vision.'

"I told my vision to the men of the camp, and they agreed that it was strong, and that I should do as the wolf told me. So I rode two days on my best horse to a stream with a forked cottonwood on the bank. I waited there until a wolf came, and I killed it.

"From the time of the vision, my name among the Cheyenne has been Running Wolf, and from that time, I have never been afraid."

Nash had listened quietly while the old man spoke. He rose and threw another stick on the fire, promising himself that he would bring the old man more wood.

"But I don't understand why you came here," Nash said. "You have no horse, no gun, and no food. What do you want?"

The old Indian didn't answer.

Nash hesitated a long moment, not knowing how to say what must be said next, and then the words came in a rush. "It's not your fault, but you are causing trouble. I don't know why, but you are. You could be hurt, or maybe someone in camp will do something he shouldn't do. Maybe it would be better if you just went away."

"I know about the trouble in this camp," the old man said. "I can smell it, but that smell does not come from me. I am not afraid.

"I would like to smoke. Will you ask the man Flynn if he has tobacco for me? Come back tomorrow night, and I will tell you why I am here."

Nash walked away from the old man's fire, an empty feeling in his gut, as though he had not eaten for days.

Uriah was already in his bedroll, and the little lean-to felt almost warm compared to the breeze kicking up outside. Nash climbed between his blankets, and for the second night, he lay awake, watching shadows play across the canvas roof until the fire died to ash.

6

Uriah had already left the lean-to when Nash awoke the next morning. The boy slipped into his clothes, pulled on his coat, and stepped out into the middle of the night. The stars were still bright, and Nash knew it couldn't be more than three thirty or four o'clock in the morning. That was early, even for Uriah.

Nash waited a few moments and then decided that his father intended to leave early. He began gathering kindling to strike a fire, but before he finished, he heard the creak of saddle leather as Uriah rode up to the lean-to, leading old Nell. Uriah didn't bother dismounting.

"No reason to wait for breakfast. Let's go."

Nash climbed on Nell, kicking her a little to catch up with his father, who was already little more than a shadow on the snow ahead. When he pulled abreast, Nash asked, "Why so early?"

"I couldn't sleep."

They rode a while further before Uriah asked, so offhandedly he gave his concern away, "What were you and that old Indian talking about?"

"He did most of the talking," Nash said, trying to be as offhanded as his father and failing just as abysmally. "He was telling me about a vision he had when he— When he was about the same age I am. He called it a spirit wolf, and he was the same color and had the same green eyes as the wolf Flynn was telling us about.

"He said his father took him into the hills, and he waited three days and nights without food or water, and he had a vision about this wolf. He said you could look into that wolf's eyes and see what the world had been and what it was going to be."

There was a question hiding in Nash's answer, and Uriah heard it. He pulled the roan to a stop and turned sideways in the saddle, his weight on the offside stirrup. His voice was low, and he seemed to be making a special effort to articulate each word. "Visions," Uriah said, "make no more sense than goblins or ghosts or witches. That boy—the old man now—was so tired and hungry and thirsty that his mind played tricks on him. If you were to stand in the sun for three days and nights without food or water, you'd have a vision, too. Only you'd dream about your classmates, or the county fair, or something like that. Our minds paint strange pictures for us to wonder at, but those pictures have no more substance than shadows on a cabin wall."

"But, Dad, there was more," Nash said. "He was told to ride two days west from the Cheyenne camp to a stream where there was a forked cottonwood and wait there for a wolf to come. He found the stream and the tree, and a wolf did come, and he killed it."

Uriah straightened a little in the saddle before speaking. "There are dozens of streams around here," he said. "Ride two days in any direction, and you'll likely stumble across one. Where there's water, there's cotton-woods, and I have yet to see a stand of cottonwood without forked trees in it.

"That old man must be close to eighty. When he was your age, these plains were thick with buffalo. Their bones are scattered from hell to breakfast around here. And wherever there were buffalo, there were wolves. Seeing that wolf he killed was just pure coincidence. Nothing more.

"Now it's different with us. We aren't going to run across that killer wolf by coincidence. We're going to have to work for that bounty money."

The two rode on. Nash was tired enough to go to sleep, but it was just too cold. He could feel his cheeks stiffen as the cold cut off circulation. He wrapped his bandana around his face, breathing through a double layer of cotton, and that helped, but it wasn't long before the moisture in his breath rimed the cloth with frost. The cold had dulled Nash's senses. It wasn't until the ban-dana took the sting from his face that Nash noticed the North Star hanging like a shard of the sun. They were traveling almost directly west. They rode another hour. Then Uriah stopped to relieve himself, steam rising from the hole he burned into the frost-lined snow. Nash got off and stretched, waiting for his father.

"We're going to drop down onto a big flat in another

couple miles," Uriah said. "There's a little creek that follows a shallow coulee back and forth across the bottom. Sometimes it almost loops back on itself. We're going to use that to hunt this fast. We will be heading northwest, so we'll have the sun at our backs. I'll be on one side of the coulee and you on the other. Just remember, if there's a coulee in front of you, follow it around until you see me. If the coulee is behind you, cut across the flat on the top and set up an ambush on the other side, waiting for me. Leave Nell back from the edge. Don't silhouette yourself. Take your time, slip down into a bush or behind some rocks and wait. Got that?"

Nash nodded, but he wasn't sure what Uriah was talking about. He understood better when they started down a long ridge to the valley floor below. It was light enough to see the general lay of the land, and Nash could mark the course of the creek from the occasional cottonwood that poked its crown over the center.

When they came to the creek, Uriah pushed the roan off a relatively steep bank, leaning back against the stirrups until his mount came to a stop on the coulee floor. He followed a little cut that meandered up the other wall until he popped out on top. Uriah waved good-bye in the growing light, and set across the valley floor on the other side at a lope. Nash kicked Nell into a walk, riding back a little from the edge of the coulee, his complete attention focused on the scene below. The coulee, marked as it was by steep walls that shaded the creek, was a world unique in itself. With adequate water, and without the baking sun, plants flourished in summer, their dried skeletons now poking out of the snow.

It was a perfect place for the wolf to hide. Casual observers from the ridges overlooking the valley would never guess the extent of the creek that lay below. The heavy brush lining the banks provided excellent cover by day, water, and the promise of game as it moved down from the ridges toward the water in the evening.

The creek bed below was crisscrossed with tracks, and whenever those tracks wove their way in and around a copse of juniper or willow, Nash would stop, shotgun at the ready, and wait to see if an animal would bolt from the cover. Most times they did, and Nash would swing the heavy double-barrel toward the movement until it proved to be a cottontail or jackrabbit or sometimes a bird. Once Nash watched as a huge white owl lifted out of a thicket with great strokes of its silent wings.

The coulee was angling generally south and it nearly touched the valley wall there before swinging back north by northeast toward the other side of the valley. Nash's mind was beginning to drift, lulled into inattention by Nell's rocking gait and his lack of sleep the night before. He would have some tales to tell when he got back to school. His teacher would probably call him up before the class and announce, "Children (emphasizing that she wasn't referring to Nash), our own Nashua is going to tell us about his adventures hunting the last wolf in the Pryor Mountains."

And then he would look around the room at all those wondering eyes and settle on Ettie, and . . .

"Nash."

His father's voice jerked him back to reality just in time to see Uriah climbing out of a juniper under the lip of the coulee rim beyond him.

"You have to stay awake, boy. I said that wolf wasn't as dangerous as Flynn made him out to be. I didn't say he would come up to you and lick your hand. You head across and set up. I'll swing around. If you see the wolf, you'll only see him for a second or two, so be ready."

Nash put the sun to his back and pointed Nell across the broad expanse of valley floor. His shadow stretched off ahead of him like a surrealist painting of a man on a horse, a long-legged, long-necked creature carrying a long-necked, long-bodied man-boy on its back.

Nash tried to pull back into himself, into the warmth of the coat and cap and gloves and boots. But even the gentle wave created by Nell as she cut through the sea of frozen air overlaying the valley floor stung Nash's cheeks and sapped his energy. He held off shivering, because he knew once he started, he would never stop— at least, not short of a fire built somewhere in the coulee ahead, its smoke signaling the end of hunting that day.

Nash guided Nell toward a cottonwood he saw poking above the coulee wall ahead. As he drew within two hundred yards of the tree, he pulled Nell up in a patch of grass scoured clean of snow at the whim of one northerly wind or another and tied her to a patch of sagebrush. She would graze there until Nash returned.

The shotgun felt heavy as he walked toward the coulee. Most times when he picked up the old double-barrel, he felt the power latent in the weapon and not the weight. But now it was weight. The weapon had become a tool to Nash, nothing more romantic than a hammer for pounding nails. He was coming of age.

He slowed his pace as he neared the lip of the coulee, taking care where he stepped to prevent rocks hidden under the snow from rattling off or sticks from breaking. He went into a crouch, not consciously but from habit. The closer he could get to the coulee before he was seen, the better his chance of getting a shot at anything that bolted from below. As he neared the edge, he knelt and leaned forward a little to peer down. He caught a flicker of movement and tensed, relaxing again as the cottontail darted out from behind a juniper bush. The rabbit was a good sign that Nash hadn't frightened the animal as he came up. That probably meant that he hadn't spooked any other animals either.

There was a lip of sandstone overhanging the creek bed and at one point, a juniper grew in front of the stone ledge. Nash decided to make that his stand. The sun was behind him, and its rays would light the coulee and confuse the vision of any animal trying to see against the brightness of the sun into the shadows on the coulee wall. He squirmed into place, hiding the sharp lines of his silhouette with the rough-edged juniper branches, and settled down to wait. Sitting there motionless, Nash waited as the cold came to him. He felt it first in his toes and then in his fingertips. Cold is a gentle lover that comes in mincing steps, teasing the edges of its chosen's senses until they no longer warn of the danger of cold's embrace. Nash struggled silently to drive the cold away, wiggling his toes and fingers to maintain circulation. His feet were beginning to hurt, a sharp pain. But Nash knew the real pain would come later.

His toes had been frostbitten before. He remembered

taking his shoes off that day at the cabin. His feet looked white, dead. But he knew they weren't dead when his mother put them in a pan of water heated on the stove. As the water did its work and the blood began to flow freely through the frozen flesh, Nash almost screamed. It was as though his feet had stored their agony, waiting for blood to cry their pain. His feet had swollen, and his toes blackened, but within a few days, he could gimp around the cabin without wincing. It was not a bad case of frost-bite, Doc Wilson said when he stopped a few weeks later. If it had been bad, Nash would likely have lost his toes, and maybe his feet.

Nash rocked his body, rolling the blood through his feet and back up his legs, willing warmth where there was cold. And suddenly he forgot the cold. His whole being focused on the flash of gray that streaked into the juniper stand below, just ahead of the rattle of Uriah's horse coming up the coulee.

As Nash rose, he eased the hammer back on the double-barrel, depressing the trigger so there would be no tell-tale click when the hammer came to full cock. But Nash's fingers were numbed by the cold, and the hammer slipped. *Ka-thump!* A cloud of black powder smoke chased the concussion into the coulee and the opposite wall exploded in white under the hail of buck-shot. The recoil sent Nash stumbling back, and he almost tripped on a low-hanging branch. But then he saw a flash as the wolf busted loose from cover, running hell-bent for invisibility promised by a bend in the coulee some sixty yards beyond. The hammer was back on the second barrel, and Nash swung that long-barreled scattergun like an instrument of fate. When the muzzle covered the fleeing animal and then swung a little ahead, Nash squeezed the trigger. *Ka-thump!* The recoil tipped up the gun's muzzle, and Nash's perspective with it. By the time he realigned his eye on his target, it was no longer there. And at that precise moment, Uriah came galloping up on the roan.

"Did you get him, Nash?"

"Don't know. Thought I had him, but I don't see him now."

"Load up and drop down into the coulee. I'll watch from up here. See if you drew blood. If he's wounded bad enough, he'll be close. If he isn't, we'll let him stiffen up and bleed before we go after him."

Nash's hands were shaking as he broke open the double-barrel and dropped two shells into the chambers, *chung,* like rocks dropped into a well. Nash cradled the shotgun in the crook of his left arm, leaving his right hand free to grasp bushes as he made his way down the slippery wall of the coulee to the bottom. He found the tracks there and followed holes in the snow that marked the animal's long stretching stride to the point where Nash had fired the shot. There was blood there, sprayed out into the snow as the buckshot coursed through the animal's body.

"He's hit, Dad. Looks to be pretty bad," Nash called up to his father.

"Get out of the coulee, Nash. Now! We'll sit up here and wait. Spook him now and who knows how far he'll run."

"I will, Dad. But just a minute."

Nash followed the tracks toward a juniper bush that hung out over the course of the creek just ahead. The tracks showed that the animal was struggling, and gouts of blood lined the trail. As Nash neared the bush, he heard a low whine. He edged sideways, training the shotgun on the noise. It was a coyote, hurt too badly to move.

"Coyote, Dad. I shot a coyote."

There was a pause, and then the sound of Uriah's voice, tinged just a little with disappointment. "Kill it, Nash. We can get a few dollars bounty and something for the hide."

Nash raised his shotgun, putting the bead on the suffering animal.

"No, Nash. Don't waste the shell. That buckshot will tear him up too much. Use a stick."

"Dad, the hide isn't worth much anyway. It's more trouble than it's worth. Why can't I just shoot him?"

"Nash, the animal's suffering. Kill him, boy. It'll be a kindness."

Nash looked around the coulee floor for a stick. He finally found a dead juniper and broke off a branch. The clean fresh scent of the wood lingered in his nose as he turned to walk to the coyote. As he approached, the animal struggled to escape, but it was too badly injured. Nash raised the limb over his head and brought it crashing down on the coyote, but a branch deflected his aim and the club struck the coyote on the shoulder. The wounded animal yelped in pain, and tears blurred Nash's eyes as he swung the club again at the coyote's head. This time his aim was true, and he heard the sickening crunch as the club drove splinters of the coyote's skull into its brain.

Nash reached under the bush and dragged the animal out. It was a fine-looking creature—its pelt was prime—but Nash noticed only the bloody concavity where the coyote's forehead had been and the macabre grin on the animal's face, its lips pulled back from its teeth in death.

As Nash stepped away from the animal, a rope sailed down from the top of the coulee and landed beside the boy. "Tie it on," Uriah said. "I'll pull him up. We'll follow the coulee until I can cross again. No sense hunting anymore around here. If the wolf ever was here, he'll be long gone."

Nash scrambled out of the coulee and walked back to get Nell. The walking warmed his feet, and Nash was thankful for that as he walked up to the grazing animal. He tightened the cinch and climbed on.

By the time Nash returned to the coulee, Uriah had tied the coyote behind the saddle on the roan. The horse was rolling his eyes, but he was well broken and ultimately put up with even that foolishness.

"Keep an eye out," Uriah said. "We might spook something yet."

Nash tried to concentrate on the coulee floor, but his mind clung to the moment when the club broke the coyote's skull. Nash had heard that sickening thump before during the summer of the watermelon.

The Brues planted watermelon each summer, not so much out of hope as stubbornness. There simply wasn't enough sun and water to grow the melons most years in Montana. But during that one magic summer, all the elements came together, and Nash watched the watermelon—just one—maturing at the end of the vine. Even in that wet year, the watermelon represented dozens and dozens of trips to the creek and back, carrying buckets of water so the plant could suck nourishment from the stingy soil.

And all that summer, Nash had dreamed about carrying the melon to the creek and leaving it there until it was cold and crisp. He knew how the knife would feel as it sliced the watermelon into thick, juice-oozing slabs. He saw in his mind's eye a chunk of bright red melon as it was raised to his lips, and the burst of flavor as his teeth crushed the melon into sweetness.

And one day Uriah put a knuckle to the melon and was rewarded with a perfect thump. Uriah and Mary watched, smiling, as Nash picked the melon and carried it toward the house. Then Nash stumbled. The melon fell, scattering blood-red fruit and black seeds over the garden. Nash could still hear the thump the watermelon made as it burst against the clay soil of the garden. It sounded just like the thump the stick made as it crushed the coyote's skull. He had cried then too.

The coulee walls were steep here, and Uriah and Nash rode for nearly half an hour before finding a place where Uriah could cross.

"We'll ride along the rims up there," Uriah said. "Make our way back to camp. Might be that we'll cut a track or spot something."

When they reached the top, Uriah pulled the roan to a stop and swung down. "Let's eat."

Uriah reached into the saddlebag, pulling out the

remainder of the roast venison from home and a loaf of bread. Nash climbed down off Nell and joined his father on a log that had long since parted with its bark. The venison and bread were an inch away from being frozen and the meat stringy, but Nash thought his sandwich was delicious. The two sat there chewing the tough meat, minds playing with the past and future. But Nash's mind soon settled on the past few days and a question that had been nagging him.

"Dad, why does that old Indian bother you so much?"

Uriah stopped eating for a moment, then he continued as though he hadn't heard Nash's question.

Despite Nash's concern that he was stepping into something that might not be so easy to step out of, the boy continued. "He's just an old man. He told me to call him Grandfather."

"Grandfather?" Uriah said as though he were talking to himself. "He asked you to call him Grandfather?"

And then there was more silence. When Uriah finally spoke, his voice was low and constrained, as though he were excising some emotion from his body, and he wanted the surgery to be as painless as possible.

"Maybe I can call him Grandfather too. . . ." Uriah said, his voice trailing off into nothingness. Nash watched his father's face and listened to the silence until he could bear it no more. Then Uriah spoke. "I wasn't sure I would ever tell you this, Nash. I wasn't sure that I ever wanted you to know, but maybe this is best.

"I never knew my grandfather. He died before I was born, before my father was grown. Grandpa and Grandma Brue died on the same day. My father wouldn't tell me how they died . . . until that night. It was an old story then, but Dad told it as though it had happened the day before, and when he finished, I understood why it was so clear in his mind.

"Grandma and Grandpa Brue came over from the old country, and they made their way west to settle with a whole colony of Scandinavians in Minnesota. The whole country was covered by trees then, big oak a hundred or more years old. Grandpa Brue worked that land like he was made of oak himself. Dad would go to bed with the sound of Grandpa's ax ringing through the woods and awaken the next morning to the same sound.

"They built their cabin from that oak. They wanted it to last forever, and I guess it did, at least for them. They're both buried along the creek, near the ashes of the cabin. Grass grows belly deep to a tall horse there, almost as though the old man is still farming the place, willing it to grow, even though he's been dead now a good many years. Grandpa was a farmer. He watered the crops with his own sweat, and they flourished. You might think a man who worked so hard for what he had would be stingy, but not him. He shared the bounty he carved out of those woods with everyone who came along, even Indians.

"From what Dad said, Grandma Brue worked hard as Grandpa did. I guess the Brues are cursed with making their women's lives hard."

Uriah's voice was dead. Emotion was gone from his face, and he continued the story as though he were repeating it from memory.

"Grandma was pretty. Dad said she had long blond

hair and eyes bright as a Minnesota lake. Grandpa was tall, rangy, with big hands and calluses hard as cowhide. Dad told me he would never forget the sound of their laughter—or their screams.

"I don't know how it started. Some said it was all over a bunch of eggs some Santee tried to steal from a farmer down at New Ulm, but it was deeper than that. The Santee had stayed in Minnesota when the other bands moved out on the Great Plains. They had a reservation along the south side of the Minnesota River. They hunted some and got an annuity, but mostly, it was hand-to-mouth.

"Still some people thought that was too much. They wanted the reservation lands for settlement. They had even asked President Lincoln to back their claims, so the whole reservation was on edge.

"Everything came apart when the Santee massacred a white family. Some men came to the farm to warn Grandpa, but he wasn't really worried. He and Grandma had been good to the Santee, and they thought they had some friends on the reservation—if whites and Indians can ever really be friends."

Uriah leaned over, his elbow on his knee. His hand was clasped tightly over his eyes as though to shield himself from the visions in his mind.

Nash thought that was the end of it, that Uriah would stop now, concede the pain was too great to continue, but just as a sigh of relief was beginning to whistle through Nash's teeth, Uriah spoke again. "And then one day when Grandpa was out in the yard splitting some kindling, the Santee came. Grandpa knew them. They had been there a dozen times before, and he wasn't worried. But something alarmed Grandma, and she sent Dad out back and told him to stay out of sight until the Indians left.

"Dad shinnied up a big oak about fifty yards behind the cabin and crawled out on a big limb where he could watch what was going on without being seen. Right away he could see there was trouble. He couldn't hear what they were saying, but he could tell there was an argument going on. Then one of those red devils stepped up and swung an ax at Grandpa's head. Grandpa was still holding his ax, and he blocked the blow. They all jumped him then and knocked him to the ground. He was stunned, I guess, and that was for the best because they started to cut him to pieces. He must not really have known what he was doing, but he kept crawling toward the cabin as though he meant to protect Grandma. He had what was left of his mind on reaching the cabin and saving his wife, and that kept him alive a lot longer than any man should have to live. The Santee were playing with him the way a cat plays with a mouse, but it wasn't until a couple of them started to skin him that he started to scream.

"Grandma heard that, and she came out of the cabin with a shotgun. When she saw what they had done to him, what they were doing to him, she turned the shotgun on him and pulled the trigger. She tried to kill herself, too, but it was one of those long-barreled muzzle-loaders, and she couldn't reach the trigger.

"So she pointed the muzzle at her chest and banged the butt against the porch. Dad said the hammers on that old gun would slip at the damnedest times, but not then, not when Grandma needed to kill herself.

"Dad was up in the tree, watching and praying the gun would go off, that he wouldn't be seen." Uriah let his breath go in one long sigh. He seemed deflated, as though his spirit had escaped with his breath, leaving him smaller, more vulnerable.

Nash was torn between his need to comfort his tormented father, and his need to hear the rest of the story. In the end, he sat quietly, waiting for Uriah to speak.

"But the gun didn't go off . . . ," Uriah said, his voice trailing off into another long sigh. "I won't tell you what they did to your great-grandma, except to say that those . . . those . . . butchers scalped her and hacked both of them up until it was hard to tell they were human. All that time, Dad was lying up in that tree, too scared to move, not knowing if he would be next.

"And when he couldn't watch anymore, he looked down, and there below, looking up at him, was a young Santee buck. Dad knew him. They had gone hunting together once. There was blood on the boy's hands, and he looked at Dad and grinned as he wiped the blood on his chest.

"Dad said it was the most evil thing he had ever seen. Then he felt warmth running down his leg, and he realized he had wet his pants. That made the Indian boy laugh, and he ran back to the cabin to help the others loot it. When they were done, they burned the place . . .

"Dad was in that tree for two days, in a kind of stupor, too scared to come down. Even after a bunch of men came to the farm and buried what they could find of your great-grandma and great-grandpa, he wouldn't leave that tree. Finally, one of the men climbed up the tree, pried him off that branch, and lowered him down.

"Dad didn't talk or eat for days afterwards. An uncle raised him, but Dad never did really settle down much, at least until he met Ma. Things picked up for him then, and it looked like everything would be all right. He was always good to me."

Tears streamed down Uriah's cheeks, but his voice went on as emotionless as ever. "We used to fish a lot, and hunt, and he treated Ma like she was royalty, but he was quiet at times, and a little moody, too. I saw that then, but didn't recognize it until I got older—until I began to see it in myself.

"Like I said, things were going along pretty well. We were farming the old place, and Dad seemed to be getting better. He would joke with folks a lot more and tease my mother till she laughed pretty as a brook running over rocks.

"He even got so he'd go to town maybe once every couple weeks and have a drink with some of his friends. They'd play whist and drink and tell lies. That's what they were doing that night."

Uriah's eyes settled on Nash, and Nash wondered again, if his father would continue.

"Mom and I were home. She was knitting something or another. I don't remember what it was now; she was always busy with something. Then Dad came in. He just kind of popped through the door. He called Ma and me into the kitchen and told us to sit down, but he wouldn't sit. He paced around the kitchen as though he was in a great hurry, but I don't think he even knew what he was doing. He told us then what happened to Grandpa and Grandma out on the farm, what the Indians did to them, and he kept saying, 'Don't you see? Don't you see?'

"Then he started to tell us what happened that night in town. He and three of his friends had been playing whist at the bar when a couple drunk Indians came in. Indians weren't allowed to drink then, same as it is here in Montana. But they knew old Jimmy Pierce. He owned the bar where Dad played cards, and he never turned down any Indian's money as long as they drank that foul whiskey he sold them somewhere else.

"Everybody knew Jimmy was selling to the Indians, but he was careful, and it didn't bother folks much. Jimmy had a bell on the back door, and when it jingled, he knew there would be one or two Indians waiting in the back room for him. He kept his 'Indian whiskey'—foul stuff that it was—locked up in a little room beside the bar, and he would pick up a bottle on his way back.

"But these two Indians came in the front where white folks drank, and that was bad. They told Jimmy they wanted a bottle. He told them to get out back, but they started to get loud. They wanted money for a bottle, the two of them collaring one man after another kind of menacing, like. Wasn't long before they made it over to the table where Dad was sitting with his friends.

"By this time Jimmy was reaching for the bung driver he kept behind the bar. He was going to toss 'em out. If Jimmy had gotten his dander up a little quicker, maybe the whole thing wouldn't have happened. Maybe things would have been different today."

Uriah took a deep breath and let it go in a long sigh. "Anyway, these two drunk bucks were standing at Dad's table, swaying back and forth like a lodgepole in a high wind. Then this one buck looks at Dad and says, 'Piss pants.'

"Dad said the rest of it was kind of hazy, kind of like he wasn't really there, like it was all bits and pieces of a dream that he was trying to remember when he woke up.

"But he remembered this. He remembered that the buck reached into a pouch on his belt and said to Dad, 'How much you give for this?'

"Then he laid a scalp out on the table, a scalp with long golden hair. It was wiry with age and the shine was gone out of it, but there was no doubt in Dad's mind it belonged to his mother. Dad said he didn't remember anything after that, not until it was all over." Uriah slipped into silence again, remembering.

"I talked to some of Dad's friends later. When that buck laid Grandma's scalp on the table, they said Dad snapped a leg off the table like most folks might break a match. He hit the one buck in the forehead with the leg and crushed his skull. The other one turned to run, but Dad reached out and caught him by the arm. The buck was trying to pull away, and Dad was trying to kill him. It was like some obscene dance, life and death high-stepping on a barroom floor. Finally, the Indian stumbled and fell, and Dad clubbed him to death.

"Everybody was kind of stunned. Dad had beaten both those men to a pulp before they could stop him. He just stood over them, hitting and hitting and hitting.

"Finally, someone shouted and Dad stopped. Kind of

like he woke up. That's when he came home and told us what happened." Uriah's shoulders were shaking, and he stopped speaking to take a deep breath, but the tears didn't stop. His voice came again as though from deep in a well, as though he were shouting from some faraway place. "Mom was crying. Just sitting at the table crying. Most often Dad couldn't stand to see her cry. If something happened that made Mom cry, Dad would drop whatever he was doing and hold her and talk to her soft-like, until he coaxed a smile out of her.

"But that night he didn't even seem to notice. He didn't seem to take much notice of me, either. He was talking like he was talking to himself, but he kept saying, 'Don't you see? Don't you see?'

"Then Dad walked out the front door the same way he had come in, no warning. He was just gone.

"Mom was sitting at the table crying, but I just didn't know what to think. It was just too much for it to sink in all at once like that. So I was just sitting there, trying to make some sense out of what I'd heard. . . .

"And then—we heard the shot. Dad was in the barn. Mom found him. She wouldn't let me go in. . . . But after she found him, she got hold of herself. There were things that needed to be done, and everything was left on her, so she did what she had to.

"Mom kind of pined away after that. She died of fever a year or so later, and I moved in with one of Dad's cousins. They were good to me, but I felt real bad. Sometimes I still do."

Some of the color was returning to Uriah's face, and he turned with what seemed to be great effort to face Nash.

"That's why that old Indian bothers me, Nash. Indians took my grandfather and my father, and I'm afraid they'll take me."

Nash sat stunned. Opening his mouth to speak seemed to take more effort than anything he had ever done. "He can't hurt us, Dad," Nash said, put in the uncomfortable position of trying to comfort his father. "He's just an old man."

"You don't understand," Uriah said. "I'm not afraid of him. I'm afraid of what I might do to him."

Nash wasn't hungry anymore. Neither was Uriah. The two repacked the saddlebags and rode the ridgetops toward camp. Ostensibly, they were hunting, but neither paid much attention to anything but his thoughts.

7

As they rode into camp, Uriah dropped the coyote off near the lean-to. A shout went up from one of the more distant tents, "The wolf. They got the wolf."

Uriah tried to wave the men away, but they wouldn't miss the chance to see "Flynn's wolf." Even Bullsnake straggled over, and it wasn't long before Nash wished he and his father had come into camp under cover of darkness.

"Well, lookee here," Bullsnake said to the little group. "We got us some *wolf* here. You shoot this wolf, boy?"

Nash tried to ignore Bullsnake, but the troublemaker persisted, playing to his audience like a man of the stage. "Come on, boy. Tell us how you shot this killer wolf." Bullsnake's voice dripped with sarcasm. "Did it ambush you, boy? Lay in wait behind a bush so he could reach out and grab you by the leg? Nah, that couldn't be it. If that had happened, you would have peed your pants, wouldn't you, boy?"

The other men were laughing and Nash looked to his father for support, but Uriah remained aloof, subdued. Nash had never felt so alone.

Flynn stepped up to Bullsnake. "This 'wolf' is damn near as good as the one you got today, isn't it?" Flynn asked. "Maybe Nash didn't get a wolf, but he sure as hell got more than you did—slivers where you sit down."

The little gathering hooted at that, too, and Bullsnake stomped off, muttering obscenities under his breath.

Nash didn't know if he should thank Flynn for his help—and risk embarrassing Uriah—or keep quiet. Nash stared helplessly at his father, and then at the Irishman. Flynn understood. He winked at the boy, but the gesture didn't hide the concern on his face. He stood there a moment while studying Uriah, perched on a log by the fire pit.

Finally, Uriah spoke, shaking loose the dark thoughts that had crowded his mind since he and Nash had talked that noon.

"Anybody see anything?"

"Nah. Nobody was out more than half a day. They know my arthritis is a better predictor of weather than the *Farmer's Almanac* will ever be. Didn't want to be caught out in a storm, so they came in early. Weather will change—and soon. You mark my words."

"If we don't cut a track or something pretty soon, we might head back," Uriah said. "That wolf could be miles from here. It might have died years ago."

"Could be," Flynn said. "Could be. I figure Abe Clark and his brother will be pulling out tomorrow, if a storm doesn't come up. You and Nash could ride in with them."

"Comes to that, we can ride in by ourselves," Uriah said a little too sharply.

"Yeah, I guess you could," Flynn said. He took one more look at Uriah's back, shrugged at Nash, and began walking back toward his camp.

Uriah slouched over the fire, bent it seemed on shutting out everyone and everything. Then Nash heard him mutter, "Oh, hell."

"Flynn," he yelled at the departing figure. "Come over tonight. We'll finish those loin steaks."

Flynn flashed a grin over his shoulder and waved his assent.

"Nash, I'm a little tired tonight. You take the horses over to the creek and water them—not too much, mind you. Then give them some oats and hay and rub them down. I'll get a fire going. Start the steaks."

Nash collected the horses' reins and led the animals toward the corral. The muscles of his legs stretched as he walked, and that felt good after a day in the saddle. Nash's eyes were focused on his feet, but his mind was miles and years away, replaying an incident that happened to people he had never even known. He really didn't feel anything at all. He knew those people from so long ago were bricks he was built of, but he couldn't mourn them, nor feel hate for the Santee. He wondered if something was wrong with him. But mostly he was worried about Uriah. Nash wanted to ease his father's pain, but he didn't know how. Uriah had kept the secret since he was a boy, feeling it gnaw at his gut. And now Nash was worrying that same question with as little success. He was still deep in thought when he heard, "Boy! Boy!"

In his reverie Nash had wandered into the old Indian's camp. It was not a place he wanted to be. He understood now why Uriah avoided Indians, and now he felt that same aversion.

"Boy!"

Nash tried to ignore the summons, but he couldn't. "Yes?"

"Come here, boy."

"I've got work to do. I can't be dallying around here."

"When you have finished your work, come here. Bring some meat and I will tell you a story."

"I think I've had stories enough for today."

"Come then. Bring the meat, and I will listen to your story."

Nash was sorely tempted. He wanted to talk to someone, but not somebody close. He needed to share those terrible secrets with a stranger, because he could never share them with a friend.

"Maybe I'll be back," Nash said, and walked on toward the corral. Before he reached the shelter of the pine grove where the horses were kept, Nash swung down to the creek and kicked a hole in the ice where it had been broken repeatedly during the men's stay at the camp. The horses drank long at the water, and Nash finally had to pull them away. The cold sucked the moisture out of all living things. It was a paradox that in the winter, with snow everywhere, more precipitation lying on the ground than most Montanans would see in a month of summer, the body craved water and food. Hunger was putting a rumble deep down in Nash's body.

Nash led the horses back up to the corral, stripped them of their saddles and blankets, and rubbed them down with hay while they ate their oats. Nothing like oats to make a horse feel fat and sassy, and they'd need that if the storm Flynn was talking about ever made its debut. After the horses settled down, Nash walked back to the lean-to. The campfire was shooting flames into the frigid air, and grease in the frying pan, perched on a rock near the fire, was already smoking.

Uriah looked up as Nash walked back into camp. The cold of the past few days had seeped into his bones, and he needed the blaze to drive the chill away. It helped, but only a little. The cold simply played hide-and-seek with the fire. If a man stood front on to the flames, the cold would slip wraithlike under his coattails and steal along his backbone and down his legs. Fires were more sacrifice than solution to the cold.

Uriah tossed the steaks into the frying pan and a little plume of smoke trailed off into the air. Nash was so hungry he thought he could eat the steaks just the way they were, just the way the old man had eaten the liver.

The old man. Nash didn't really want to deal with the old man now, not with Uriah frying steaks, not while Uriah was hanging on to the routine of cooking meals as a drowning man clutches a rope thrown to him. But before long, Flynn came over. Flynn had the Irish gift of healing pain. He bantered with Uriah, weighing the hurt hiding behind the forced smile and light talk. The Irishman examined the pain, as a doctor might examine a tumor, searching for its weakness. Then Flynn lanced that hurt with humor, gently at first, opening it a bit more with the whiskey he brought with him. Nash watched until he heard his father chuckle. Laughter wasn't a cure, but it sutured the wound Uriah had opened that afternoon.

When Nash heard his father laugh, he walked over to the burlap sack where the deer carcass was hanging. "Dad, I'm going to take the old man some liver."

Flynn saw the tension between Uriah and Nash, and he put his words between them. "I don't know. Looks to me like Nash is more worried about passing the liver off on somebody else than he is about feeding that old man."

And Uriah returned Flynn's grin. "Maybe so," he said.

The old man was sitting beside the fire, still as death. Nash didn't know how anybody could sit like that without moving. But that was foolish. He had to be moving. He had to be going down to the creek for water and back into the trees to relieve himself. Sometimes a man could ignore a call from God but never a call of nature.

Nash held the liver toward the old man, and the knife appeared again from beneath the robe as he took the meat. He impaled a piece of the liver on the willow stick Nash had cut the night before and began roasting the meat.

"We've got some bread in camp. You could have some of that."

"This is all I need."

While the old man was eating, Nash walked over to the woodpile by the grove of trees, gathered an armful of firewood, and returned to the fire.

"Don't know how you can keep that fire going. Never seems to be any wood around here," Nash said.

"Plenty of wood around here," the old man replied.

Nash sat on a rock across the fire, watching the Indian finish off the liver, warmed barely past thawing. As the old man chewed, Bullsnake came huffing up.

"My, my. Ain't this cozy, though. A coyote killer and a stinking old buck. Must be you got a touch of injun in you, boy. Quality white folks can't stand the smell of injuns."

Nash was tempted to point out that Bullsnake had precious little knowledge of "quality" folk, but he kept his peace.

"You're real lucky," Bullsnake continued. "Weren't for this boy here, you'd be starving by now. Maybe he just don't know any better, but the rest of us do. You remember that, old man."

Nash glanced at the old man. He sat there as though Bullsnake's words held no significance. But the old man's hands had disappeared under the buffalo robe again, and one of those hands held a wicked-looking knife. Bullsnake might be getting himself into something he couldn't handle.

"Yup, I thought by now you might be getting a little light on meat and be moving on, old man. That wouldn't bother anybody, except maybe our young injun-lover here. But then he goes out and shoots a killer coyote. You injuns love to eat coyote, don't you, old man? You want I should cut the liver out of that killer coyote and bring it up here and *feed* it to you? You want I should do that? Maybe you want some of the coyote, too, boy? Maybe injun-lovers eat coyotes and dogs, just like injuns?"

Nash was mad, but scared, too. Bullsnake was talking himself into something and Nash didn't know what. He did know that if Bullsnake laid a hand on Nash, Uriah would step in. Nash didn't want his father put to a test like that—not now, not today. So he sat like the old man, quiet and unmoving.

Then Bullsnake strutted off. The old man turned to watch him go. "He is wrong," the old man said. "Only a coyote would think of eating another coyote." The wheezing began again, and Nash wondered if the old man was laughing or having trouble breathing.

"What makes Bullsnake like that?" Nash asked.

"What makes the Northern Lights?" the old man answered. "They are both creations of the earth. I understand neither of them, but that is not important. On this earth, I must only understand myself and God."

"That's what Dad said, too."

"Your father is obviously very wise," the old man said, the wheezing beginning again.

"Are you afraid of Bullsnake?"

"No. Only Bullsnake is afraid of Bullsnake. A rattle-snake that buzzes at shadows is no trouble for a man with a stick. We are Bullsnake's shadows."

Nash threw another piece of wood on the fire, watching the sparks shower upward from the embers there. "Dad told me a story today," Nash began while the

118

old man was still chewing his dinner. "It was about some people he knew back in Minnesota. They thought the Indians, the Santee Sioux, were their friends, but the Indians killed them. Butchered them."

Nash stopped talking, leaving the question he hadn't asked hanging in the air.

The old man had draped the robe over his head again, and his face was lost in the deep shadows of it. But Nash could see the glint of his eyes, almost hidden under heavy brows and darkness.

"It was war," the old man said. "When I was a young man, we won horses and honor in war. But the white man taught us there is not glory in war, only death and hunger and pain and hate. Many of the white man's ways were mysteries to us, but we came to understand his war very well."

"The white man never taught the Indians to torture and then butcher their victims," Nash said, his voice rising. "We didn't do that."

"No, you didn't teach us that. As children, we would catch prairie dogs or rabbits and cut or burn them a little at a time until they were dead. Those with skill—those who could make the animal or man suffer most before they died—were greatly honored.

"One time on the Greasy Grass, we caught five Crow. They fought bravely, but we soon killed all but one. He towered above the bodies, fighting even though he knew he would die. So we told him that we would honor him for his bravery, that we would not kill him if he came with us, and he did. He walked alongside our horses, joking with us.

"But we soon found an anthill, and we staked him to the ground and his head was on the anthill. Then we scalped him and cut off his eyelids, his nose, his lips and his ears, and then we left him there. The ants were crawling on his eyes and he couldn't even blink. But just as we promised, we didn't kill him." The wheezing started again.

A shudder ran through Nash. "How can you laugh at something like that? It's—it's . . . evil."

"You find that evil?"

"Yes," Nash said.

The old man sat quietly, putting white man's words in order in his mind so Nash would understand what he was trying to say. "When we were put on the reservation, I thought about all that had happened, and I wondered at it. My people, the Cheyenne, were dead, sick, or imprisoned. The buffalo, the seeds of our life, were gone. From herds as many as the leaves on the cottonwood trees, they were gone to some place we did not know. Some people said they walked into a hole in the ground, never to return while the white men walked on the earth. Mother Earth is thick with white men. They are as ticks on a cottontail in spring, and like the ticks, they suck the juices from Mother Earth, killing her, killing us.

"And I wondered at that. I wondered what had happened that made it so, what had happened to the medicine of my people. So I went to see the blackrobes, and I said, 'Teach me of the white man's God, the one they call Our-Lord-Jesus Christ.' I listened to them and asked questions, as you are asking questions now, and I learned from the Holy Book. So when you speak of evil, I know what you are talking about. I didn't know before. There was no evil before the white man came.

"We killed our enemies very slowly and very painfully, but we didn't know that was evil in the eyes of the white man's God. But the white man killed us very slowly and very painfully, and he knew what he was doing was evil. Are we, then, more evil than the white man?"

"Lies!" Nash cried. "You are lying to me, old man. We didn't torture you. We didn't cut you up while you were still alive. We didn't kill you the way you killed my great-grandmother and great-grandfather!"

Nash had half risen in his anger, but then he sank down again to his seat by the fire.

The old man took his eyes from the fire and focused on Nash.

"The white man does not torture? The white man gave us blankets filled with pox. Have you ever seen a village stricken with the pox? First, it kills the young and old. Mothers and fathers watch their children die. Wives watch husbands die, and husbands wives. The pox is a bad way to die. It sets the body on fire and consumes the spirit as the fire consumes these logs. In the end, there is nothing but ashes. The pain of dying is a terrible thing to watch, but the real pain comes later, for the living.

"Then the white man gave the Indian alcohol, trade alcohol mixed with tobacco and pepper and death, but we wanted it more than we wanted our honor. It has been years since the white man first gave the Indian alcohol, and still we suffer long, slow, painful deaths.

"We have no food and no way to get it. The buffalo are

gone. We are beggars now. We didn't even know what begging was before the white man. We cared for each other. There was great honor in giving to those in need. But now there is nothing to give. Our lives, our honor, our people, our lands, and our beliefs have been taken from us. We die slowly, in great pain, and the white man laughs. He laughs at the drunken Indians and the light-fingered old bucks. The white man is much better at torture than we ever were."

"It isn't the same," Nash retorted. "It isn't the same as what the Indians did to my great-grandparents."

The old man continued as though he hadn't heard Nash. "My wife was called Antelope Dancing. She was graceful, like the antelope, moving over the earth without effort. There are hard edges to the way most of us walk, but not Antelope Dancing. I would find her sometimes, staring at the horizon as though she were thinking about how long it would take her to run to it, beyond it, to see what she had not seen.

"Magpie was my son. We called him that because he chattered all the time. He was always underfoot. Wherever I went, he was there, watching me. Antelope Dancing said he would sometimes cry at night when I was gone. That was his mother in him. I . . . loved her very much.

"Spring Flower was like the sego lily in spring, shy, face down, bobbing with the winds, delicate yet full of life and beauty. I always marveled that I was part of the creation of such beauty. She was our first.

"One day I left them in the early morning to go to the edge of the camp to relieve myself. As I was walking, I saw a flash on the hillside above the camp, and then the sound of long guns. The soldiers had come in the night. We didn't expect trouble because we had a paper saying we were good Indians, but they didn't ask to see the paper.

"I turned and was running toward my lodge when the cannon shell hit. Those white men did not torture my wife. That first shell turned her into a fine pink mist, like part of a rainbow, but they tortured Magpie. He was still alive when I reached him. He was trying to crawl away, but he had no arms and only one leg. He was crawling like a caterpillar, arching his back and pushing himself with his leg. He didn't go very far before he died. I was very glad to see my son Magpie die. . . .

"I found Spring Flower leaning against a rock, looking down at what was left of her body. She asked, 'Why?' and then she died.

"The Cheyenne were good at torture, but the white man is much better."

Tears came to Nash's eyes. "I'm sorry."

"I'm sorry, too."

"It was the war."

"Yes, it was the war."

Nash stared down at the snow, hiding his face from the old man, but he looked up when the old man spoke. "Tell me about your great-grandfather and grandmother."

"I better get back to camp."

"Tell me."

And Nash did, hesitating at first, and then the words came in a torrent. And when Nash was finished, the old man said, "And now your father dreams of his father as

I dream of Antelope Dancing and Magpie and Spring Flower. We have both been strong under torture. Tell your father I am sorry. We are of two people. And there was a time when our people came together like two streams in the mountains, raging against each other, but in time we will be one people, and nobody will be able to tell one stream from the other."

"Nash, time to eat." Uriah's voice floated into the old man's camp, breaking the spell there.

"I've got to go," Nash said, rising from the rock where he had been sitting.

"Tell your father what I said," the old man called before returning his attention to the ghosts flickering in his fire.

Uriah and Flynn had already eaten. Nash found a tin plate and slapped a couple of steaks, charred on the out-side and dry as dust on the inside, next to a heap of beans still steaming from the pot on the fire. He wolfed down his food and looked at Uriah.

"Go ahead, boy," Uriah said to the unspoken question. "We've had all we want."

Flynn chuckled. "Only living thing I've ever seen eat like that had four feet and pulled a wagon. If he grows the way he eats, you'll be able to hook him to the plow, Uriah."

"Could be he'll eat the plow, too," Uriah retorted, while Nash dumped the remaining beans on his plate and finished them. The two men were waiting for Nash, cleaning their teeth with the chewed ends of willow splinters. Nash rose, gathered the tin plates and scrubbed them in the snow.

"I put a pan of water on," Uriah said.

Nash nodded. He would run the plates through the hot, soapy water to cut the grease and then dry them by the fire. As Nash busied himself with his chores, Flynn pulled an envelope from under his coat. "I hope you don't mind, Uriah, but I couldn't help saving the best for last. It's a letter from Mary."

Uriah looked up in surprise. "How did that woman manage to get a letter up here? I swear she could hitch a lightning bolt and ride it to the moon if she had a mind to."

But the tremble of Uriah's hands belied the lightness of his words. He took the letter from Flynn as though it were something fragile, precious, cradling it in his hands a moment before tearing it open.

"Ulysses sent George Dunn out to check on some stock," Flynn said. "He was close to your place, so he stopped in to see how things were going. Mary was out on the creek chipping ice with a crowbar and a bunch of sheep gathered around her like kids waiting their turn at a lemonade stand. George pitched in on a few chores, but she was doing fine, just fine."

"So George just happened to be there?" Uriah said. "If you see Mr. George Dunn before I do, you tell him he's owed. You might mention to Ulysses, too, that he's going to have to build better fence if his stock had taken to wandering that far off his range."

Flynn's face crumpled into a reluctant grin, and he tried to defend himself, but Uriah wasn't listening. He was holding the letter flat against the light of the campfire, trying to pick words off the page. He read through the letter twice before he held it out for Nash. "Something in here for you, too, Nash," Uriah said. "She's doing fine, just fine."

Flynn grinned. Probably wasn't anybody in shouting distance who didn't know that Mary Brue was "doing fine, just fine."

Nash bent closer to the fire, squinting at the pages in the soft, flickering light.

Dear Uriah and Nash:

I know you are safe. God just wouldn't let anything happen to you, but I'll admit it scared me this morning when I saw that rider coming up the lane. I thought he was bringing bad news, but then I saw it was George. If it had been bad news, Katie or Ulysses would have come.

I know it's silly to worry, but it's hard not to. Next thing I know, you'll be like Jake Chambers, telling the neighbors how your "tetched" wife is carrying on.

George chipped a hole through the ice on the creek for the sheep and hauled up a little hay for me too. It's funny, but I've been thinking that you'd be home by the time the hay was gone. I felt funny having George build up the feed stack, like I was telling you to stay away. Maybe you should talk to Jake after all.

The house seems hollow at night without you, and I bump around the empty corners like a bee in a fruit jar. It's times like that when I would give a year of my life to have the two of you home again.

But I don't want you to quit something you've

started. I don't want you always wondering if you might have been the ones to get the wolf, if things might have been different if you had.

Nash, don't let your father do anything foolish. He isn't a spring chicken any more, even though he does strut around and squawk like one.

Please be careful. Know that I am perfectly well and praying for your safety and success.

Love,
Mary

Nash grinned as he finished reading, but there was a shadow on it. Caught up in the excitement of the hunt, Nash hadn't considered the burden left on his mother's shoulders. He passed the letter back to his father, who folded it and slipped it inside his jacket. Nash could see the guilt on his father's face, too, plainer in the firelight than the words of the letter.

The three sat in silence, watching the flames dance through the air. Uriah was the first to break the stillness. "If we had known George was going past the place, I would have written Mary a letter."

"I know you would," Flynn said.

There was another long silence before Uriah spoke again. "That Mary. She's a lot stronger than she looks. She can do most anything a man can do. It might take her a little longer, but she can do it."

Flynn interrupted the next stretch of silence just before it snapped. "I was talking to Mose Adkins today, just before he pulled up stakes. Funny old goat, Adkins is. Said he didn't feel right, thought something was coming he didn't want to be around to see. Said it has something to do with the old Indian. Told me he knew the old man before."

Flynn paused for effect, and when he knew he held his listeners as tightly as the letter had a moment ago, he continued, "Adkins got a ranch just off the Cheyenne reserve and he knows some of the Cheyenne pretty good, at least some of the younger ones. He hires them for haying or branding or whatever. Says they make good hands.

"One day he was over at the Two Bellies place to ask Chester to come over the next day, but he could see as soon as he rode up that he had stepped into something.

"Old Two Bellies, Chester's grandfather, had taken real sick that night, and the family thought he was going to die. Chester and his sister—they both had schooling at the mission—wanted to take the old man to the agency. But their grandmother wasn't having any of that. She figured the doctors would cut up Old Two Bellies the way he cut up the troopers in the Custer fight.

"Adkins was watching the whole thing. Oddest argument he ever saw. Chester and his sister were laying it on thick and heavy in Cheyenne, but the old woman wouldn't say anything at all. She just glared at Adkins once in a while.

"All of a sudden, that old man over there in the buffalo robe was standing behind Adkins. The Two Bellies place is right out on a ridgetop. There isn't any cover between there and the Crazy Mountains, but all of a sudden our old man was there, just standing there like he had been there all the time. Adkins said it kind of spooked him.

128

"It kind of spooked Chester and his sister too. The Cheyenne believe that old man can travel through the air. They really believe that. Seems our old man is some kind of shaman or something.

"Well as soon as the old man showed up, Chester's grandmother starts chattering away at him in Cheyenne, but he just waves her away and talks to Chester.

"Chester is spooked. He's shouting at the old man in Cheyenne, and he jumps on his horse and lights out like the devil is after him.

"The old woman starts keening. Adkins hears that and asks Chester's sister what the hell is going on. She is crying, and she says her brother will die, that the old man said so.

"By this time Chester is at a high lope. He's going down the ridge toward the bottom, but all of a sudden his horse spooks at something and jumps right off the rimrock, eighty feet straight down, with Chester hanging on to the reins like that's what he meant to do.

"Adkins yelled for everybody to get his wagon, and he runs the rig down there, holding back from the edge as best he can. He pulls the wagon to a stop and they all go look over the rim. Chester and the horse are down below, broken up real bad, and neither of them moving. By the time they get down to him, Chester is dead. Adkins said the fall must have killed him right away.

"When they get back, they hear something in the cabin, and they find our old man singing over Two Bellies and blowing sage smoke at him. Whatever it was, it worked. Two Bellies is still alive, and Chester has been dead for some years now."

Nash said, "How could the old man have known that Chester would die?"

"He didn't," Uriah said. "He just planted the idea in Chester's head and the boy's imagination did the rest. Just goes to show you how dangerous superstition can be."

"But Chester had been to school," Nash objected. "He didn't believe in those old superstitions."

"Chester had learned to read and write, but he was still Cheyenne."

"But how did the old man show up without anybody seeing him coming?"

"It's just another one of those stories, Nash. The reservation is full of them. They don't mean anything at all. I think you'd better turn in. Likely we'll have a busy day tomorrow."

8

Morning came early and cold. Nash lay in his bedroll, shivering, in dread of leaving the warm blankets. He took a deep breath and plunged into the cold, pulling on his trousers and shirt with shaking hands. He bent over, pulled on his boots, tied a double knot, and stepped out into the false dawn.

"Why'd you let me sleep so late?" he asked Uriah, who was already drinking coffee brewed over the campfire.

"Thought maybe we both needed a little extra. Seems like we've been at this a long time."

Nash nodded and ate and began his chores. Uriah

waited by the fire, sipping coffee while Nash scrubbed the plates clean and put the cooking gear away.

"Flynn was by this morning. Says his hands are hurting bad. He thinks it's going to storm, but then he's been saying that for the last two days. Thought we'd give him the benefit of the doubt, though, and not go out so far."

Uriah climbed to his feet, pitching the dregs of his coffee on the fire, and Nash followed his father to the makeshift corral. The horses were bunched together, their breath hanging over them in a cloud. Flynn was there, leaning against a tree, watching something or someone hidden from the Brues on the other side of the horses.

As Uriah and Nash approached, Flynn looked up and grinned. "King of the West is getting ready to do some hard riding," Flynn whispered, nodding his head.

Bullsnake was there, gathering his gear. Nash hadn't realized that anyone could look awkward getting bridle, saddle, and blanket in some reasonable juxtaposition, but Bullsnake was doing just that. And while the horses were clouding the air with their breath, Bullsnake was turning it blue with his words.

When his gear was arranged to his satisfaction, Bullsnake stepped into the corral, slipped a lariat over his horse's neck, led the gelding to a tree, and tied him up. Then Bullsnake ducked through the rope that edged the corral, picked up his saddle blanket, and ducked back under the rope to return to his horse. Once the blanket was in place, he returned for the saddle, grunting a little as he ducked under the rope again and once more as he lifted the saddle to the back of his horse. Saddle in place and cinch tight, Bullsnake untied the horse and started to lead him to the section that served as a gate.

"Bridle!" Flynn yelled at him. "You forgot the bridle."

Bullsnake looked up, startled that he was being watched. "I didn't forget any son-of-a-bitching bridle," he said. "I was just bringing the horse over closer to it."

"Some people put the bridle on first," Flynn retorted, his wide grin obvious to Bullsnake even across the corral.

"Some people get their noses all busted up because they can't help poking them into other people's business," Bullsnake retorted. "And if I wasn't so busy, I might come over and explain that to you."

Nash made the mistake of snickering, and Bullsnake turned ugly. He stalked across the corral and pulled up short in front of Flynn.

"If I want any shit out of any of you sons-of-bitches, I'll squeeze your heads," he growled, daring any of them to say anything.

The gauntlet had been thrown, and Nash thought Bullsnake needed it thrown back in his face. But Uriah and Flynn were silent, and Bullsnake sneered.

"If you ladies will excuse me, I'll be going," he said and walked back across the corral to his waiting horse. He slipped the bridle on, again a little awkwardly, and led the animal out of the corral.

He climbed on, and with a great sense of drama, raked the animal with his big, ugly Spanish spurs. The horse had a sense of drama too. The gelding stood up on his hind legs, as though he was meant to walk that way, and for one sickening moment, Nash thought the animal would fall backward on his rider. Bullsnake had very little to recommend him as far as Nash could see; still, Nash wouldn't want a horse to fall on anybody. But Nash had overestimated Bullsnake's riding ability: he slid off the back of the horse like rain off a tin roof. The horse crow-hopped over the packed snow, and Bullsnake, all wild-eyed, ran for his life.

It started as a chuckle, and burst into a guffaw, Flynn, Uriah, and Nash laughing head-back, belly-deep laughs. Bullsnake started cussing in earnest, unwrapping a whole lexicon of expletives that Nash had never heard before and wouldn't likely hear again. The gelding had stopped bucking, and Bullsnake grabbed the dragging reins and jerked the horse's head around cruelly. Then he mounted, and holding his heels well off the horse's flanks, yelled, "Giddyup!"

Flynn actually had tears in his eyes, and Uriah was holding his stomach. Nash looked at the two of them and began laughing all over again.

"Ah, it was worth getting up late," Uriah said wheezing. "I needed that more than I need any scrawny old wolf, five hundred dollars or not."

Flynn couldn't talk. He was still chortling, and Nash with him. When the laughter finally died down, Nash and Uriah began readying their horses. After Uriah and Nash mounted, Flynn called them over.

"You might be a little careful," he said. "Bullsnake won't take kindly to this morning, and he'll come at us. Not head-to-head, but he'll come at us."

Uriah and Nash nodded, and the two rode out of camp

heading a little more north than east. The ride was glorious in the early morning light. Most of the world was white, with ribbons of blue marking the gentle convolutions of the earth and the shadows of pine, sage, and juniper. Whatever was not white or blue was black. The eye shut out the flash of the sun and made silhouettes, startlingly clear silhouettes, of everything else.

"If Bullsnake could have just laughed this morning, he wouldn't have gotten so mad," Nash said.

"If Bullsnake had laughed, he wouldn't be Bullsnake," Uriah replied.

"Looks like Flynn's rheumatism is wrong again. It's warming up. We might even have a chinook coming in."

But over the next hour Nash noticed the bite had come back to the air.

Uriah kept the same general north by northeast course, hugging ravines and stands of pine for cover, and finally, as they were nearing the top of the long ridge that ran roughly parallel to their path, Uriah pulled his roan to a stop and climbed down.

"We're going to go over the top as quiet as we can," Uriah whispered, "and take a peek over the other side. Stay low."

The hill was steep and slick with snow. The last fifty or sixty feet, Nash had to grab the branches of juniper bushes to keep his balance. Once he slipped, the branch he was holding broke under his weight, *crack!* Uriah scowled and motioned for Nash to be more careful.

By the time they reached the top, both were puffing, and they stopped a moment to catch their breath. The air was redolent with the scent of pine, and Nash couldn't remember ever having seen a more brilliant day.

The ridge was the edge of an ancient bed of sandstone that had broken in a long-past convulsion of the earth's surface. As the ridge had risen, the adjoining slab of rock had settled into a wide valley. Over the years, wind and rain had cut into the exposed sandstone, leaving ridges and coulees leading to the valley below. The shady sides of the coulees were thick with pine and fir, while the sun-ward slopes tended toward juniper.

Uriah studied the scene below, trying to think as a wolf might. A wolf would want cover that would allow him to travel from water below to the ridgetop without being seen. He would want to be near game trails and the brushy cover that mice and rabbits made their homes. But Uriah's conjecture couldn't narrow the scope of the hunt. There were miles and miles of country that fit these criteria. Finding the wolf would, after all, be an exercise of the legs and not the mind.

"Nash, I'll move up the ridge, and you move down. Keep back out of sight, and watch for trails. We'll scout it out today and hunt it tomorrow. Be ready just in case."

Nash nodded. He broke open the action of the double-barrel and dropped a couple shells into the breech. He had walked only about fifteen feet when he saw it.

"Dad," Nash whispered, trying to keep his voice down and relay the urgency he felt at the same time. Uriah looked back, and Nash waved him over.

Nash hadn't really seen it at first, but the blue shadow where there shouldn't have been a shadow drew his eye back to it. The track was in the snow next to the line of rock brushed clean by the wind playing along the edge.

135

Uriah saw it, too, and he knelt to examine the track. It was huge, five or six inches across, and clear in the skiff of snow.

"Three toes," Uriah said. "A three-toed wolf. I'll be damned."

Uriah rose and stalked along the rim, searching for a sign indicating where the wolf had abandoned the bare rock for snow. Once the animal stepped into the snow, they could track him, come back and get the horses, and run him to the ground.

Uriah's heart was beating faster. He had stepped up to a higher plane of consciousness that only the predator and the prey know. He heard a scramble in a tree fifty yards away. It was a tiny bird hopping from one branch to another. Uriah's vision was so sharp that he could identify individual feathers on the bird's breast. He could hear each of Nash's measured breaths, and the thump of the boy's heart, too.

Even so, he almost missed the point where the wolf next left sign. A snow-laden bush had been touched enough to shower its load on the bare rock. There was only that, nothing more, but it was enough to stop Uriah, to focus his attention.

"Down there, Nash. See that little lip sticking out of the rim? Yeah, there. About fifteen feet down."

The wolf had leapt off the top of the rim, aiming for the little ledge. He barely made it, and once he was there, the tracks revealed that he had scrambled to find purchase on the tiny sanctuary. Had he fallen, he would have dropped twenty-five feet to the rocks below. But he hadn't slipped.

"There, Dad. See the juniper bush?"

Uriah nodded. The wolf's next leap had carried him into a juniper bush growing from precious little soil in a crack in the rim, and from there, the wolf had jumped to the ground. There was no way for Nash and Uriah to get down the rim. The rope was back with the horses. And from the top of the rims, there was no way to know which way the wolf had run. He could duck under the overhang of the giant slab of rock and travel for miles absolutely invisible to anyone above.

Uriah shook his head in frustration. "He must have heard or seen us," he whispered. "Or he wouldn't have risked a jump like that. He's safe now. No way to get to him with the horses, and without the horses, we'll never see him again."

Uriah sat back on his haunches and turned his attention to the valley floor below. There was something wrong. The valley was disappearing into a sea of ice crystals that marked the approach of Arctic air. And out of that sea came deer, straggling into long fearless lines like perverse lemming marching away from the sea. Over the deer a flock of birds swirled about, a living gray cloud carried on some unfelt capricious wind.

The animals seemed oblivious of everything but the need to find cover. They walked out of the mist overtaking the valley below like ghosts, their fear of predators revoked by the storm. Storms were the most vicious predators of all, and no respecters of either hoof or claw.

In the stinging cold, Montana was a hell's Eden where predator and prey alike ran from the killer cold, seeking shelter, seeking life.

"They're bunching up, Nash. There's a storm coming, a bad one, and they're bunching up."

Uriah was up and running. He yelled for Nash to follow. Nash could barely hear his father. The wind was keening now, in anticipation. He ran along the edge of the rim where the snow didn't impede his steps. It wasn't far back to the horses, but Nash knew the trail stretched from life to death.

And then they were there, taking deep gulping breaths of frigid air into their lungs. The horses were nervous, jumpy, and when the Brues mounted, both animals wheeled around and put their tails to the wind. Uriah pointed them south-southwest and kicked the horses into a trot.

"We have to try to get back to camp before the snow hits. Keep close. Don't let me out of your sight."

It was a race against the elements, and the elements won. There were just a few flakes at first, zipping past like stones from a sling. Then the wind picked up, and the world disappeared. There was only Uriah and Nash and the horses and brutal cold. Mostly there was the cold.

The wind played hide-and-seek across the two hunters' backs, seeking chinks in the layers of clothing laid on like armor. When the wind breached the wool and cotton, it crept forward like a line of skirmishers, leaving the flesh cold and dying in its wake. The cold was the veteran of many battles and never had it lost an encounter. The victim fled to the cover of a cave or teepee or cabin and survived, or the victim died.

Nash and Uriah were fleeing now, Uriah occasionally

pulling his compass from his pocket to set their general direction. They had been lucky so far. The wind had held relatively true, and the horses' instinct to run before it had kept them moving toward camp. But they were traveling blind. Sometimes Nash would feel Nell lunging up a hill or brushing past a copse of trees and think, This is where we skirted the top of that coulee, or, This is the hill where we first saw the ridge. But each time, he shook his head in disbelief. They had to be farther than that. If they weren't, they couldn't make it, not in that cold.

The wind screamed at them now. It tore the breath from Nash, and he wrestled with it so that he would not suffocate. But each time he stole a breath from the keening wind, it seared his lungs with cold.

Nash's feet and hands hung unfeeling from his arms and legs. There was a certain relief in that; at least he didn't hurt so much. He was tired now, and he wanted to sleep for a while, take a nap on Nell's back. There was no harm in that. Nell would follow the roan anyway. The roan! Nash didn't know where the roan was. He hadn't seen the horse or his father for some time. The implications of that were beginning to sink in to his mind when Nell rocked to a stop. A nagging thought crept into Nash's mind. If Nell stopped, he would die. Suddenly, he was very, very frightened. He must find his father, or he would die. His fear chased away the somnolence the cold had brought him, and he knew, crystal clear in his mind, that he must make Nell move. Nash screamed and kicked the horse in the ribs, harder than he had ever kicked anything. She plunged ahead and down—and foundered.

Nash knew he was dead then. He had committed the unpardonable sin. He had panicked for a moment in a Montana snowstorm, and now he was dead. Nell had smelled the trap. She couldn't see through the stinging wind any better than Nash, but she knew the coulee ahead of her had drifted shut with snow. She knew if she tried to cross it, she would founder in the drift and die. She didn't know the same way Nash knew he was dead, but she knew nevertheless. Still when Nash raked her sides with his heels, she jumped willingly enough. Old habits die hard.

Nash got off Nell, sliding into snow up to his armpits. He struggled like a man trying to pull himself from his own grave. Death would take him, but only after a fight, feeble as that might be. He tried swimming through the snow back to solid ground, paddling and kicking with dead feet and dead hands, but he was only sinking deeper. It seemed warmer, somehow, buried away from the wind. Maybe he would sleep for a moment, rest up before trying again. Nash closed his eyes and the world disappeared into nothingness.

Uriah had allowed the roan to have his head when he came to the snow-filled gully, trusting the horse's senses over his own instincts. The roan hesitated and then turned at right angles to the wind, following the edge of the hidden gully to its head.

Uriah knew his trust in the horse was well founded when the roan turned his back to the wind again, holding true to the same rough compass reading they had been following. It was at that point that Uriah felt compelled to look behind him, to turn his face into the stinging wind to search for Nash. Uriah didn't understand that compulsion any more than he understood the roan's decision to turn away from the hidden gully, but he didn't hesitate to follow its dictates, searching the white, shifting land for the hazy shape that would be Nell and Nash. It wasn't there.

Uriah waited a moment for Nash to appear. He *needed* to have Nash appear. Uriah didn't want to face the obvious any more than he wanted to face the stinging wind.

If Nell had stepped off the trail, if she went down, or if Nash slipped out of the saddle, he would likely be lost forever. Even now in this frigid, godforsaken wind, Nash might be lying in the snow out there, stiffening in the cold as the wind covered him.

Uriah yanked the roan's head around. The gelding fought the reins, reluctant to turn into the wind. Uriah fought the panic he felt. He wanted to gallop screaming into the wind, shouting for his son, his only child. But he knew that would mean death for him and Nash, so he gritted his teeth and leaned into the wind and the desperation he felt.

The roan's tracks had disappeared almost on the horse's heels, hidden by that screaming, evil wind. But there were still tiny drifts marking some of the tracks, clues the wind had left to lure him back to death. Uriah followed them until they turned at right angles to the wind. They disappeared then, but Uriah followed the gully, marking its edge by the way the roan shied whenever he neared it. Uriah was watching the edge, face turned away from the wind, when the roan stopped.

There, through the wind and snow and the fear, Uriah saw Nell, foundered in snow over her shoulders, and beside Nell, a small dark object lay motionless in the snow. *Nash!*

Uriah fought off the urge to leap after Nash. That would come later, when all else failed. But for now, Uriah took the lariat off his saddle, tied a loop in one end with numb fingers, and threw the loop toward Nash. A gust of wind took the loop and carried it away from Nash, teasing him.

He pulled the loop back and threw it again, and again. He was trying very hard to control the panic he felt. Uriah didn't know if Nash was alive or dead, he didn't know if Nash was dying while he watched. But he knew the only hope he and Nash had now came from his ability to reason. He must remain calm. He threw the loop again.

Nash was asleep when something struck him on the face. He didn't know what had awakened him, but then it seeped into his consciousness the way the cold had seeped through his clothes. It was a rope: his father had thrown him a lifeline. Nash slipped the loop over his head and chest and under his arms. Uriah backed the roan, and Nash slipped out to the edge of the coulee. It was so easy, and it had seemed so hard.

Uriah helped Nash to his feet. Nash could see fear in his father's face, hear it in his father's hoarse voice. "Nash, stamp your feet. Turn your back to the wind and stamp your feet."

Nash did as he was told. There was an unreal quality to the exercise. He was stumbling more than running in place, his frost-dead feet striking frost-dead ground. The movement set his heart pumping faster and the muscles of his legs helped force warm blood through his feet. The deadness went away a little, and his feet began to ache. That was a good sign. Maybe he would live. Maybe he wouldn't lose his feet.

Somehow the pain was therapeutic. His mind focused on it, and he almost forgot that awful, cutting, killing wind. Nash took his mittens off and put his hands under his armpits in his jacket. Moments later, his hands began aching, too. But perhaps more important, the pain was pulling the cobwebs from his brain. He was beginning to think again, and at that point, he recognized his father's face just inches away from his own.

"Nash, I've got to go into the drift after Nell. I'm asking you to back the roan when I call out. You've got to do it, boy, or I'll never get out."

Uriah turned and plunged into the snow. He pushed, scrambled, swam out to the stranded horse and dropped the loop of rope over her head. Then he grabbed the reins and scrambled back. He needed to be out of the way when Nell tried to do what he would tell her to do.

"Haw, Nell! Haw!" Uriah yelled against the wind, tugging the horse's head around with the reins. At first Nell stood motionless. But she could no more ignore Uriah's commands than she could ignore the call of nature. She had leaned into harness too many times.

She began lunging, struggling to do her master's bidding. She was actually beginning to turn, even while sinking deeper in the snow. Uriah didn't dare put pressure on the rope now. It might break her neck, but if he didn't . . .

"Back the roan! Easy, Nash! Easy!"

Uriah didn't know if he had been heard above the screaming wind, but the rope tightened, and Nell was coming around. It was critical now. The horse was almost at right angles to the rope. If she fell, she might not be able to get back on her feet, but she lunged again, and her feet caught the lip of the coulee.

"Back, Nash. Take up the slack."

A minute later, Nell was standing in snow at the edge of the coulee, sides heaving, and Uriah was yelling again at Nash. "I don't know where we are. I'm going to take Nell's reins so we won't drift apart again, and I'm giving the roan his head. If he takes us back to camp, we'll be okay."

Nash knew his father had left the sentence unfinished. If the horses didn't take them to camp, if they wandered aimlessly, Nash and Uriah would pay with their lives. But there was no choice.

So they rode, rode on for hours, days, it seemed. The wind played hide-and-seek with their bodies, finding warmth wherever it hid and snatching it away.

The awareness that he was once again dead was rising in Nash, but he refused to give in to even so obvious a fact. Whenever he could muster the energy to raise his head, giving the wind a new angle of attack, he would see his father hunched on the roan like a boulder in a stream of swirling white water. He couldn't die with his father watching—he didn't want to be a disappointment—so he held on to his life and wouldn't let go. That was the hardest thing Nash had ever done. It took all his body's energy to keep his blood flowing. He tried to listen to the sound of his heart, knowing that when it quit, he could stop this pretense of life and sleep. His father couldn't blame him if his heart just quit.

On they rode, bodies slumped in their saddles, bound for wherever the horses chose to take them, betting their lives that the horses would take them to safety before they died.

Then the animals stopped, Nell almost bumping into the roan. It must be over now. There was no need to keep up the pretense any longer. Nash was so grateful, and he closed his eyes to sleep, only to awaken to the sound of someone screaming in his face.

"Nash, we made it. Flynn set up a windbreak for the horses. Climb down, and we'll get them taken care of."

Nash climbed off the horse with no sense of relief, only the dread that the ordeal was not over yet. Still, it was a little better on the ground. Uriah had opened the corral, and Nash led Nell through.

Flynn had stretched a web of tarpaulins through the trees edging the windward side of the corral. The wind screamed its fury at being denied full access to the warm flesh of the horses there, but the tarpaulins held tight to their lashings, and the animals were bunched and reasonably comfortable.

Uriah filled buckets with oats for Nell and the roan and carried in the two buckets of water Flynn had left by the corral. As cold as it was, there was only a skiff of ice on the water. Flynn must have waited for them at the corral as long as he dared.

When Uriah had finished, he took some rope lying beside the corral and tied it with clumsy, frostbitten fingers end to end with the ropes he and Nash carried in their saddlebags.

Nash was standing in the lee of the tarps, stamping his feet, when Uriah walked up. "We're going to tie this to that tree, and then walk in the direction we think the lean-to is. If we don't bump into it, we can hang on the rope and swing back and forth in arcs till we find it. We have to be careful. We could still get lost, and we won't last much longer without shelter."

Nash nodded. "What about the old man, Dad?"

"What do you mean?"

"Without shelter, he'll die too."

"Indians are accustomed to this weather. He'll pull through."

"No man could live through this storm without shelter, Dad."

Uriah bowed his head to shield his face from the wind and the snow. Then he looked at Nash. "We're bunching up, aren't we boy? Predator and prey and we don't know which is which. We'll try to find him on the way to our lean-to, but we better move fast. We don't have much time."

9

Nash's body was racked by the cold. He clenched his teeth to keep them from rattling against each other. Stepping back into the fierce wind from the corral windbreak took a major effort of will.

Uriah and Nash marched along an azimuth estimated by Uriah before they left the corral, guided by compass and paying out rope behind them. Their dead reckoning worked, but still they almost bumped into the old man before they saw him. He was still sitting on the log, with his back to the wind and the buffalo robe pulled over his head, shut tight against the elements.

Uriah reached out tentatively and touched the old man on the shoulder. At first there was no movement, and Nash thought the old man might be dead, but then the robe shifted a bit, leaving a narrow tunnel leading back to the glitter of the old man's eyes.

Uriah was shouting over the wind, and it appeared that he was screaming at the old man, venting some great anger.

"You better come with us," Uriah said. "The storm will kill you."

"You do not want me dead?" the old man asked.

"No, I do not want you dead," Uriah said in a voice so soft that Nash almost didn't hear him.

The old man nodded and rose. He stood swaying for a moment against the wind, and Uriah reached out and took the Indian's arm. Uriah shot another azimuth, and the three of them lurched through the snow blindly following the needle on the compass, paying out more rope, but more slowly now, moving in an expanding arc from the corral toward their camp.

The navigation was more difficult this time and the men missed. They didn't know if they had gone too far or not far enough. They didn't know if their straight-line distance from the corral was correct or incorrect, so they began swinging in wide arcs, hanging on to the rope. Each time the group slowed, stopped, and headed back into the wind, Nash found it more difficult. The wind tore mercilessly at him, but he gritted his teeth to stop the shaking. He trudged on, one foot after another.

And suddenly, woodenly, they were there. Nash stood, leaning against the wind, until Uriah took his arm and pulled the boy down into the lean-to. It was cold there, too, but there was no wind, and compared to outside, it seemed almost warm. That illusion was enhanced when Uriah lit their kerosene lamp with shaking hands and hung it from the top brace of the lean-to. The lamp swayed back and forth as the wind buffeted the canvas, casting mellow light and deep shadows.

"Nash, get out of your boots. Take off everything but your long underwear."

Nash tried to do as he had been told, but the knots he had tied that morning were too cunning for his numb fingers. The old man reached out and took Nash's feet. He unlaced the boots easily and slipped off the two pair of heavy wool socks Nash was wearing. Then, by the light of the swaying lamp, the old man examined Nash's toes and feet. He pressed the flesh. It turned white under his touch.

The old man traced the width and depth of the frostbite with his fingers. Still silent, he reached for Nash's hands and repeated his examination there. Before reaching for Uriah's feet, the old man looked into Uriah's eyes for a long moment. Still Uriah jerked when he felt the old man's touch, and his body tensed as the old man probed the extent of Uriah's injuries.

Running Wolf reached for a rawhide bag he had carried with him into the lean-to, and the buffalo robe slipped for a moment from his face.

Nash saw the old man's face more clearly than he had before. It was much darker than Nash remembered, and more heavily eroded by the runoff of the juices of youth. His hair was white, banded here and there with darker shades of gray, and braided into two strands that disappeared into the robe over his shoulders. The bones of his face pushed his wrinkled skin into a terrain as sharp and broken as the prairie on which he lived.

If the old man's face lacked the fineness of bone and skin of Europe's aristocracy, it was compensated with the regalness with which it was carried and the intelligence that glittered in the deep black eyes.

The rawhide bag contained a salve of sorts, made—if the substance could be judged by smell alone—from some kind of animal grease, perhaps bear.

"You will not lose your feet or hands," the old man said. "But you must warm yourselves now."

He took the lamp from the center pole and placed it on the floor of the lean-to. He motioned for Nash and Uriah to scoot, blanket-draped, close to the lamp, feet, hands, and spirit gathering warmth from its pale light.

"You must wait now for the pain."

The wait was not long. The pain came as the cold had, an animal of prey creeping stealthily into toes and fingers. Uriah and Nash had stopped shivering. The lean-to was cold, but without the wind that howled its disappointment outside, their bodies had begun to warm within the sheath of blankets. They were warm enough to sleep, and they would have, but for the pain.

"Why does it have to hurt so much?" Nash asked through gritted teeth.

The question was rhetorical, Nash's attempt to reach into his mind and pry it away from the pain, and for a moment it worked. Then the old man grabbed Nash's attention, pulling it away from his pain.

"If it were not for pain," the old man said, "man would have nothing. All other things were created by God and belong to Him. Only man's pain is his own."

"Our luck is changing, Nash," Uriah joked. "We just struck the mother lode."

The old man began wheezing again, shoulders shaking as he laughed soundlessly.

But when Uriah turned to the old man a moment later, there was no laughter in his eyes. "Why are you here?"

Running Wolf paused, straightening his shoulders a little. "I came because the wolf called me. He told me it was time."

A ripple ran through the hairs on the back of Uriah's neck as the old man continued, turning to Nash. "This is the wolf that led me to the spirit lodge when I was a boy and gave me my name. He has called me on the wind many times since then, and always I have answered. You do not hunt a wolf. You hunt a spirit."

"That's crazy," Uriah said. "Spirits don't leave tracks in the snow. This wolf is huge, but he's a wolf, nothing more and nothing less."

"He is a spirit wolf. If you saw his tracks, it is because he wanted you to."

The old man peered deeply into Uriah's eyes, and Uriah felt helpless, lost in the depths of those two dark pools.

"The spirit wolf has been with my people always. He was with us in the fight with the white man. Many times I called to him for strength and courage, and always he was there. . . .

"We fought the white man, and he killed the buffalo. We warred against the bluecoats, and they burned our villages. We fought until hunger caused our bellies to rub against our backbones. When we could no longer bear the cries of our children, we stopped fighting. We stopped fighting to fill our bellies."

The old man gazed at Uriah. No emotion cracked that rough visage, but Uriah knew the old Indian was speaking from great pain. "The spirit wolf hungers for nothing but justice for his people, so he continued to fight long after we gave up. He has learned from the white man: it is better to war against buffalo and cattle and let hunger war against men. So he stalks the prairies, killing cattle and leaving them for his friends, the coyotes and the magpies."

Uriah shook himself free from the old man's gaze, but he felt no relief, only a growing sense of dread. The old man was obviously insane, haunted by the spirits of his people. He was insane and armed with a long-bladed knife, and he was sitting less than an arm's length away.

Uriah began probing the extent of the old man's madness as the old man had charted the frostbite on his and Nash's feet and hands. "You said it was time, old man. Time for what?"

The old man pulled the buffalo robe tightly around his shoulders again and stared for a long moment at the kerosene lamp.

"Once I thought the buffalo were so many that they would always feed my people, but the white man killed them in the span of a young man's life. Once I thought the white men were so few that we could kill them all, but now they are more than the buffalo were."

The old man spoke of killing dispassionately, and that frightened Uriah more than if he had shouted his madness at a world changed beyond his ken. There was a deliberateness to the old man's insanity, and the muscles of Uriah's back tensed as the story continued.

"The people of the reservation are changing. The young are taken from their homes and told that the way of the white man is better. They laugh at the old ones. They laugh at me. When I have gone, there will be no one. So the wolf called to me. I stepped away from the reservation and ran here on the wind. That is my real name, not what the white men call me on the reservation. I am Wolf Runs on the Wind."

"But your people aren't here, old man. Changing or not, your people are on the reservation. You should have stayed there."

"My people are here. Can you not hear them in the

wind, keening their deaths? Can you not hear them weeping at what has come to pass?"

The old man stopped again and looked deeply into Uriah's eyes. "There were people who lived on this land before my people spilled out on the plains to hunt the buffalo. When we came, they moved on. I have often wondered where. Perhaps they went into a hole in the ground with the buffalo. I am an old man, waiting my turn. You have nothing to fear. You are safe with me tonight."

As Uriah listened, the muscles in his back tightened, as though his body were readying itself for flight. Uriah knew the old man was insane, but yet that part of the mind that still dances in shadows thrown on cave walls played with the hairs on Uriah's neck.

"What makes you think this is your spirit wolf?"

"I have seen this wolf. I saw him when I was a boy about to become a man. I saw him when the trapper took him to Billings. I heard him in that iron cage, crying out his anger and his pain, so I ran to him on the wind. I wept in my heart to see him so humiliated. But I watched and I waited. I was there that night he fought the giant dog. And afterward, I felt each blow the trapper struck. I felt the rope tighten about the wolf's neck, choking off his life. I felt each jolt of the wagon as the trapper carried him to his cabin.

"So I ran there, too. I was waiting when the trapper came. He was still crazy. He pulled the wagon around the cabin, and I wondered how he would unload the wolf. He did that as he did all things—cruelly. He tied a rope to the cage and then tied the other end to a tree behind. He whipped the horse, and she lurched ahead, pulling the wagon out from under the cage. It fell with a great crash, and for a moment, I thought it would break. But it held, and the trapper laughed, a wild crazy laugh. He poked the wolf with sticks, torturing him, and danced around the cage as though he were crazy. I would have killed the trapper, but for that. I did not want to kill a crazy man.

"The trapper was up late that night, drinking whiskey and goading the wolf. Then he went into the cabin. I listened until I heard him snoring, and then I walked up to the cage. Spirit Wolf watched me. He knew me. Whenever the trapper took the canvas off the cage in Billings, the wolf would search the crowd for me. I was always there.

"I opened the cage, and the wolf thanked me. I thought he would go into the cabin then and kill the trapper, but he walked down along the creek, waiting there to see if the trapper was crazy enough to follow. The next morning when the trapper saw the wolf was gone, the smell of his fear almost made me gag, but the trapper followed because he had to, or live in fear for the rest of his life. I saw him walk to where the wolf was hiding, and I watched the wolf kill. I felt his teeth slit the trapper's soft belly, and I smelled the trapper's guts spilling on the ground. I felt the wolf's happiness while he watched the trapper die. He was so happy, I wanted to laugh. We both waited until Flynn came, and then we ran away on the wind, laughing together at the joke we had played on the trapper."

The old man began wheezing again, and the sound of

it made Uriah's skin crawl. "How can you laugh at something like that?"

But even as he asked, Uriah knew the answer. He couldn't apply rational standards of behavior to the old man. The old man lived in an irrational, insane world.

The old man looked at Uriah, his eyes glittering in the lamplight. "Because I laughed, I no longer hated the trapper. There are things I cannot laugh at. They hurt me deep in the heart. I cannot laugh when I think of my woman and the children. And you cannot laugh when you think of your father and your grandparents, so it is best that we laugh at the things we can."

"Old man," Uriah said softly. "The wolf is not a spirit wolf. He does not speak to you, and you did not run here on the wind. Your mind is old, and it plays tricks on you."

"Maybe," the old man said, reaching again for Uriah's feet. His toes were black, bruised by the ice crystals in the flesh. The flesh was swollen, too, stretching the skin tight. The old man put more salve on Uriah's feet and hands and then on Nash's. "Your feet and your hands will be sore in the morning. It is best that you do not walk much, but you should move your fingers and toes."

Then he stopped for a long moment, his head down, with the long, white braids drooping past his face.

"You must remember this, boy," he said, without looking up. "You must remember what I have said to you. You are seeing the passing of a time. There is no one left to remember this but you. It is important that you know what you see. I am an old man. I know of the white man's heaven. I know of the white man's God, the great

155

goodness that He is. The blackrobes taught me. But I would not fit in the white man's heaven. People would hold their noses and tell me they can't stand the stink of Indians. In the white man's heaven, I would be alone. My father and mother would not be there. In the white man's heaven, I would be Light-fingered Old Buck. I am Wolf Runs on the Wind.

"The wolf grows weaker as I do, and lonesome for the spirit people. When I die, there will be no one for him to call in the night. There will be no one to listen to his loneliness on the wind. You ask me why I came here. I came to see the wolf die. I came to see the passing of another time on this land, and my heart is on the ground."

And then the old man began singing. His voice keened with the wind. It spoke with an emotion he denied himself in the telling of his story, and tears came to Nash's eyes. The sound was as primal as life. It drummed in Nash's ears, and he felt himself carried by its beat. He felt the pain and loneliness of the old man, and his resolution, too. Finally the old man was quiet.

"What were you singing?"

"I was singing of what has been and what will be."

Wolf Runs on the Wind reached beneath his robe, and Nash remembered the ugly knife hidden there. The old man slipped the strap over his head, pulled the still-sheathed weapon out, and handed it to Nash. "I will have no need for this. I would like you to have it. Perhaps it will help you remember that once I was here."

The old man lay down, and in a moment the soft sound of his breathing filled the lean-to.

Sleep did not come so easy to Nash. He lay in the lean-to with the smell of smoke and sage and pine and thought about what the old man had said. He was still thinking about it as he fell asleep.

I came to see the wolf die.

10

Nash awakened the next morning with a start. Something was wrong, but he didn't know what it was. Light! It was light, and he hadn't milked Bess. Why hadn't his father called him? He would be late for school.

But Nash's first movement under the blankets brought him back to reality. The pain in his feet and hands spurred his mind. The storm and the night with the old man came back to him in bits and pieces, building in patches until he remembered all. But just to be sure he wasn't dreaming, Nash opened his eyes.

The lean-to was empty, and cold, still smelling of smoke and sage and pine. Nash slipped out from under the covers and raced the cold to get dressed, but he lost. His feet and hands were puffy and weak. Forcing his swollen feet into his boots with weakened hands required great effort. He tried to tie his laces, but the resulting knots were big and loose, and Nash knew they wouldn't hold if he had to do any serious walking. He prayed that he wouldn't have to.

The cold outside took his breath away. Uriah and the old man were sitting beside the fire. They had built a heat reflector on the other side of the flames, and as Nash came nearer, he felt the warmth. He settled down on a log beside his father.

"Cold," Nash said.

"Flynn says it's forty-five below zero this morning," Uriah replied. "But there's no wind. Thank heaven for that."

"Anybody caught out?"

"Just us." Uriah reached for the coffeepot, pouring the thick, steaming liquid into his cup. He handed the cup to Nash. "Might warm you up a little."

Nash took the coffee gratefully. He didn't particularly like coffee, it was too bitter for his taste, but this morning it was nectar of the gods.

While Nash was sipping the coffee, Uriah pulled the cooking utensils out of the canvas sack and set the frying pan to warming over the fire. The store of sidepork was almost exhausted, and Uriah held what was left in his hands a few moments, weighing its importance before filling the pan with meat. A minute later, the pork was frying in its own grease, and Uriah was liberally sprinkling the spattering concoction with salt and pepper.

"That's it," Uriah said, passing the slices of meat around the fire. "No more sidepork. But we've got enough bread left to make this a meal."

The bread was frozen almost solid, and Uriah's knife stuttered its way through each slice. The old man waved the food away at first, but Uriah insisted, and soon he was dabbing the bread in the grease with as much enthusiasm as the other two.

The enthusiasm ended a moment later with the arrival of Bullsnake. "Heard you got caught out in the blizzard," he said directly to Uriah. "I always knew that farmers were stupid, but that takes the cake. You should look to getting yourself a new papa, kid. This one's dumb enough to kill you."

Nash was watching his father's eyes, but Uriah seemed intent on the fire.

"Is it time?" Uriah said softly without looking up.

"Time?" Bullsnake asked. "I don't know what you're talking about. I just came over here because my nose was itching. I wanted to know why that was."

"And now you know?"

"Yeah. The smell comes from a dirty old buck and two injun-lovers. You stink up this camp, Brue—you and your kid and your Sunday-go-to-church act. You figure this old man is your key to the pearly gates. That's bull-shit, Brue, and so are you. I don't like you, and I don't like your kid, and I don't like this old man. You and I are going to tangle, but not today."

Bullsnake stood wide-legged, watching his words bump against the silent group by the fire. "Why aren't you laughing now, Brue? Last time I saw you, you were having a good old time at my expense. You don't think I'm so funny now, do you, Brue?"

Bullsnake turned to Nash with a sneer. "Your daddy's bullshit, kid. You stick around him long enough, and you will be too. He'll keep you around and work you to death if you let him, and beat you to death if you don't. You can't count on anybody or anything, kid. You'll just get kicked in the teeth."

The old man spoke from across the fire. "Is your father not dead?"

"Yes," Bullsnake said. "He's dead."

"You waste your time fighting with a dead man," the old man said.

Bullsnake jumped as though he had been struck. "Old man, I didn't even know you could talk until just now. It would have been a lot better for you if I had never found out."

Bullsnake started for the old man, and Uriah rose to meet him.

"Stop!" The voice was low, raspy and cold. William Maxwell was standing there.

Nash remembered what Flynn had said that first day: *"Watch out for him. He's about half crazy, and he's handy with a knife. Bullsnake struts his stuff when Maxwell's backing him up."*

But this time Maxwell wasn't backing him up.

"We've got a wolf to kill," he said in the same cold raspy voice.

Bullsnake moved for the first time since Maxwell had spoken. "You're lucky, old man. You, too," Bullsnake said, nodding at Uriah. "But your luck won't hold long after I get back. If I was you, I'd pack up and get out of here."

"If I were you," Uriah said, "I'd practice keeping my mouth shut."

Bullsnake reached down as though he were going to pick up something heavy, but when he straightened, there was nothing at the end of his arm but a fist headed for Uriah's jaw. It didn't complete its journey, blocked in midswing by Maxwell's "No! Later."

Maxwell turned his back on the scene and walked away as though there were no question in his mind that

Bullsnake would obey, and Bullsnake did, muttering warnings to Uriah about what would come.

The three were quiet for some time, and then Nash spoke. "Are we going out this morning?"

"No," Uriah said. "We need the rest, and the horses do too. This snow is just like powder. If a little wind came up, we'd be caught in a ground blizzard. I'm not ready for that. Are you?"

Nash shook his head.

The old man, hidden again in the folds of his buffalo robe, spoke. "The blizzard is over. It will begin warming this afternoon. But you should rest for a few hours and stay warm."

"How can you tell it's going to be warm?" Nash asked.

"Can you not feel it?"

"All I can feel is a fire in front and a cold behind."

The old man began wheezing again, and Nash was pleased that he had made Wolf Runs on the Wind laugh.

Uriah was still grinning, as he stood and stretched in the frigid air. "Going to give the horses another look-over and some more oats," he said.

Uriah walked toward the corral as though he were being very careful not to crush the snow beneath his feet. He favored his toes as he walked, taking his weight on his heels. It appeared that he was walking on stilts.

"Your father is a good man. If we had won the war, he would have made a good Cheyenne. But we would have been forced to keep him on the reservation for a few years until he learned our ways."

The old man chuckled again, but Nash didn't. He had never considered the Indian reservations in that context before, and the idea captured his imagination.

"Your father is a man. He *knows* what is possible and what is not. So when I tell him that the spirit wolf calls to me on the wind, he knows that it cannot be so. When I tell him that I run on the wind, he knows that this is also not true. So your father thinks that I am either a liar or a madman. I should be content that he thinks me mad."

The old man's voice was coming once again from the depths of the buffalo robe, muffled and soft, so Nash moved closer to hear more clearly.

"Once Colonel Dodge took some of my people to see an iron horse. But when they got there, they saw this thing made of steam and smoke and iron and wheels. They watched, waiting for it to do some tricks, but it did nothing but roll up and down the track. We were ready to go home. Everyone was disappointed because we could see no magic in the iron horse.

"But then one of the railroad men stepped up to one of the tall poles that carries the talking wires. The man put his belt around the pole and climbed it. We put our hands over our mouths. Now, there was magic!"

The old man shifted on the log, and Nash could see the glitter of his eyes again. "We were not yet ready then to see the magic of the iron horse. It was beyond our understanding. Maybe the spirit wolf is beyond your father's understanding."

The old man's voice grew even softer. "And maybe God made the spirit wolf because I was not yet ready to see what He is. I have wondered about that since the time I spent with the blackrobes. Sometimes, I think I can only see the man climbing the telegraph pole. . . .

"Your father knows these things are impossible, so he does not listen and think about them. I leave that to you, boy, as a gift along with my knife. I must go back to my camp now. The time is very near."

Nash watched as the old man shuffled back to the fallen log at the edge of the camp, brushing it free of snow and sitting down to wait. Nash was still watching the old man when the shout went up from the other side of the camp. His heart sank as he looked up. Bullsnake and Maxwell were riding into camp on the far side, and draped across Bullsnake's saddle was the wolf.

Until that moment, Nash hadn't realized how important the wolf had become to him. He didn't know yet why that was. The images ran together: the irrigation ditch his family needed to survive; his mother, sitting at the piano, looking at her hands and weeping; Ettie watching as he rode home in triumph; his father's terrible secret; the storm, Bullsnake, and the old man. He couldn't understand how they all fit together. But he knew somehow that he and his father and the old man were linked to the wolf.

The old man was still sitting at his camp. He hadn't moved. Maybe he was as stupefied as Nash. Maybe he could not understand what had happened either.

Uriah stepped into camp. His face was empty, ashen.

"Let's go see."

Nash climbed numbly to his feet. They hurt so. So did his hands. He seemed to hurt everywhere, hurt and be numb at the same time. He felt pain in each step as he walked across the camp to the gathering of men surrounding the gloating Bullsnake.

"It's all in knowing what the hell you're doing," Bull-snake was saying. "We figured there was no sense going out while all you amateurs—farmers," Bullsnake spat, with a nasty look at Uriah, "was out fooling around. We figured that we'd let you get this old wolf running, keep him from killing for a few days, and force him out in the open. So we waited, sitting in camp all nice and comfy, while you did our work for us."

Through it all, Maxwell stood at the edge of the group, saying nothing, face hidden in the shadow of his wide-brimmed hat.

But Nash was paying no attention to either of the men. He had eyes only for the wolf. It was marked as Flynn had said: mostly white with a band of dark fur around the eyes and back toward the tail. The animal wasn't nearly as large as Nash's imagination had painted him. He was tall, but skinny, and his hide was mangy, with no luster. Hairs around the muzzle were white with age.

Without realizing what he was doing, Nash walked up to Bullsnake's horse. He reached down and took the wolf's right front foot. Three toes! This was the old man's spirit wolf, all right.

"You want to look at this killer wolf, farmer boy?" Bullsnake asked. "Have a gander, but don't get too close. You been around that old buck, and my horse spooks at the smell of Indian."

Bullsnake laughed his mean nasty little laugh, as he untied the rope. The wolf's still-warm carcass slithered off the horse and fell to the ground. One of the men in the crowd reached down and stretched the wolf out.

Nash could see the animal had been magnificent once,

but he had long since passed his prime. Nash couldn't imagine how the scruffy old beast had survived in the wild.

"Pretty good shot," Flynn said. "Right between the eyes."

"Wasn't much," Bullsnake snorted. "He was running about two hundred yards away, and he made the mistake of looking over his shoulder. With me on the rifle, he didn't have a chance."

"Where'd you get him?" Flynn asked.

"Big ridge, north and east of here," Bullsnake said, so pleased with the attention he was getting that he even winked at Nash.

But Nash wasn't thinking about Bullsnake.

"A big ridge north and east of here. . . ." Bullsnake and Maxwell must have hunted the ridge where Nash and Uriah had seen the track. They had been just a day too early. That one day had nearly killed them in the storm, and now Bullsnake and Maxwell were here with the wolf.

"I meant, where did you get the wolf before you staked him out on that ridge?" Flynn asked quietly.

"What are you saying?" Maxwell hissed.

"I'm saying that this isn't the right wolf, and if this animal hasn't been penned, I've never seen one that was."

"You calling me a liar, old man?" Bullsnake snarled, and for the first time, he frightened Nash. Bullsnake came up on the balls of his feet, fists clenched at his side. Maxwell was edging around the group when Flynn spoke again.

"You've got a helluva gun, Bullsnake, to leave powder burns on an animal at two hundred yards."

"Maybe I exaggerated a little," Bullsnake said. "So what? This is the wolf, exactly as you described him. The marking is the same. He's missing a toe on his right front foot. Personally, I don't much give a damn what you think. You can't prove this isn't the wolf. He's just aged a little. You should know about that better than any of us here, except maybe for that old buck."

"He's marked the same," Flynn said. "But I'll bet that dark mask wouldn't hold up in a heavy rainstorm."

Bullsnake snarled and lunged for Flynn, but Uriah stepped in between the two.

"And old or not," Flynn continued with an eye on Maxwell, "I've never known an animal to grow another set of teeth in its old age."

Flynn reached for a deerskin bag hanging from a leather thong around his neck. "I told you the first night you were here about that time in Billings when the wolf killed that big mastiff and ran up the wall of the auction arena to take a swipe at ol' Charley. He missed Charley's throat, but he cut his arm to the bone.

"Nobody else noticed, but I saw that the wolf had stuck one of his fangs in the arena wall. I took it with me, and here it is."

Flynn opened the sack, dumping the contents into his left hand. Then he held the fang up between his thumb and forefinger. It was broken off cleanly, and no one could know how long the whole tooth was, but the portion in Flynn's hand was enough to set the imagination working. Long it was, and thick as a woman's little finger. The years had yellowed it, but still it held a sense of threat and majesty, too.

"A tooth," Maxwell whispered through gritted teeth. "Nobody told us about any damn tooth."

Bullsnake chimed in. "Nobody told us that because it ain't true. Flynn likes to play games, and he's trying to pull a fast one on us now."

Warming to his subject, Bullsnake's eyes swept the crowd, searching for support from the watching men. There was none.

Then another man spoke, someone Nash had seen but not met before.

"This wolf," he said, pointing at the animal on the ground, "looks a lot like one I saw one time in that dog and pony show over by that hot springs on the Clark Fork. Except for that black mask." He reached down and rubbed the dark hair on the wolf's head between his fingers. They came away black.

Flynn's voice was thick: "Bullsnake, you and Maxwell better be out of here by early tomorrow morning. No later."

"You ain't telling me nothing," Bullsnake shouted, but Maxwell's "Shut up!" stuck like an exclamation point at the end of Bullsnake's speech.

Maxwell stalked off, Bullsnake following on his heels. Bullsnake walked about fifteen feet, then turned and sneered at the group. "There isn't any killer wolf, anyway. Those stockmen just wanted to put on a show. Do you think they'd offer five hundred dollars if there really was a wolf out there? You're like a bunch of dumb son-of-a-bitchin' sheep." Then he turned on his heel and followed Maxwell.

Nash looked up. His father's face was wooden. He nodded toward their lean-to. They walked back together, not talking, feeling a strange sense of futility that weighed down every step.

"Let's build up that fire a little," Uriah said, pitching on a couple of logs.

"Want me to get some more wood?" Nash asked.

"No, I don't think we'll be needing it."

"The old man didn't move, Dad. How do you suppose he knew that wasn't the wolf?"

"Wrapped up like he is in that buffalo robe, he probably didn't even notice the fuss. If you were to go over there and ask him about it now, he'd probably say, 'What wolf?' "

"We'll be going, won't we?"

"Yeah, I think so. Lot of work to be done at home. We can't leave that hanging on your mother. I'd like to take a look at that ridge one more time, see if we could pick up any tracks, but it would most likely be a waste of time."

"Do you think that was the wolf's tracks?"

"Might have been. Big as a horse he was, to leave tracks like that."

Nash held his hands out to the fire's warmth. "Dad, I'm real sorry."

"Yeah, son, I am too."

They were quiet then, looking up as Flynn walked into their camp, snow squeaking beneath his feet. He settled down on a log without speaking.

Finally, Flynn broke the silence. "Bullsnake and

Maxwell have pulled out their celebrating whiskey. They're sitting over there now, getting drunk and mean."

"That was a dumb stunt with the wolf," Uriah said.

"I imagine those two have been called damn near everything but smart," Flynn snorted.

"Nash and I are thinking of leaving, maybe tomorrow."

"Lot of people are. Bullsnake and Maxwell kind of took the fun out of it."

"Is that what we're doing, having fun? If this is fun, Mr. Flynn, I wish you had been along with Nash and me in the storm. That would have been a real knee-slapper for you."

Both men chuckled.

"You know what I mean," Flynn said.

"Yeah, I know. But there's not much magic in it anymore."

"Not much," Flynn agreed. "What do you say we put a real cap to this, have a big blowout tonight. Maybe you and Nash could go get a deer and we could eat steak and maybe I could rustle up a drink or two."

"Sounds good. Know any likely areas close by?"

"There's usually a bunch wintering around a spring about a half mile west of here. If you come up on them real quiet, you should be able to get one easy enough. They're pretty accustomed to seeing men on horses.

"It might do Nash a lot of good," Flynn said, staring into Uriah's eyes so the emphasis would not be missed, "to get out of camp for a while."

Uriah nodded. "Can't go anywhere until tomorrow, anyway. Come on, Nash. Let's go shoot us a deer."

Nash's fingers felt stiff and awkward as he saddled Nell, and he had to wrap the cinch around his hand to pull it tight. It was then he noticed Uriah watching him.

"Mine, too," Uriah said.

They rode east, walking the horses, working the kinks out of strained muscles and tender fingers and toes.

"It's warmer, just like the old man said," Nash said.

"It's warmer anyway," Uriah said. "Suppose there was just as much chance it would be warmer as anything else. You know what they say: Only fools and crazy people predict the weather in Montana."

"It seems funny he didn't come down to see the wolf."

"The old man? Probably just didn't strike his fancy. Indians seem to do things pretty much by impulse. If he wasn't like that, he wouldn't be here. He'd still be on the reservation where he belongs."

"Do you suppose he knew it wasn't the real wolf?"

"Nash, you're making more of that old man than there is. His mind is all tangled up with the years. There isn't any more to it than that."

"The wolf is really important to him, and he didn't even come down to look. Seems he would have done that, if he hadn't known that it couldn't be the right wolf."

"That's the way it seems, but that isn't the way it is."

"What will happen to him when we leave?"

"That's up to him, not us."

They rode a few moments in silence, and then Uriah pulled the roan to a stop, twisting in the saddle to study Nash.

"You aren't planning to take him home, are you, boy,

like a stray puppy?" Uriah's face broke into a grin. "I'd dearly love to see the look on your mother's face if you brought that old man home and said he was moving in with us. Whooee! That would be a sight to see."

Nash was glad to see his father laugh. Uriah was still smiling as they came to the coulee Flynn had described. Uriah shifted his weight in the saddle, studying the lay of the land.

"Now, if we were to hunt this right," Uriah said, "we'd probably get off here and walk along the other side, hoping we'd spook something up one way or another. But the way my feet are feeling right now, I'm not about to climb down in that cold snow. So we'll go horseback up this ridge to the top and come down the other side. What with the storm last night, they'll be coming out a little earlier than usual. We'll just take our time and watch for them."

The horses slipped and stumbled a couple of times as Uriah and Nash prodded them up the ridge, but they reached the top just moments later. The two worked along the edge of the coulee, staying back from the lip, riding up periodically to scan the patches of timber below for moving deer. They had nearly reached the head of the coulee when Nash noticed a flash of white near a juniper bush.

"Dad, there!" he whispered, slipping off Nell.

"Yeah, I've got him. Good eyes, Nash."

Uriah knelt, sitting back on the heel of his right foot and bracing his left arm on his left knee. A shell snicked into the chamber; Uriah laid his cheek on the comb of the rifle stock. Then he dropped the hammer to half cock and leaned back from the weapon.

"He hasn't seen us," Uriah whispered. "You want to take him?"

Nash shook his head, and Uriah leaned over the rifle again, thumbing the hammer to full cock. Nash knew as he watched the deer below that his father's finger was tightening on the trigger.

Uriah squeezed.

Crack!

The deer leapt at the shot, bouncing up the far side of the coulee, seeking sanctuary. It nearly reached the top before its legs crumpled under it, and it fell, slipping back down the hill until it lodged in a juniper bush.

"Got him in the lungs. Didn't dare try for a neck shot at that distance."

Uriah was smiling. "Can't complain about a deer like that. Ran right up the hill for us. Saved us a lot of trouble."

Uriah marked the spot where the deer had fallen and mounted the roan. Nash was quick to follow. The two rode around the head of the coulee about a quarter mile above and swung down the other side to the fallen deer. When Uriah spotted the gnarled pine that marked his firing point on the other side, he stopped, looking ahead for the rock outcropping that resembled a stern face. There it was, and below, just where it should be, was the blood-streaked trail, where the deer had slid down the hill.

Uriah pulled a rope off the roan, and Nash followed his father down the hill. The hill was steep and slick, and Nash slipped more than once, sliding down on his backside until his boots found purchase against a rock or a bush.

The deer was dead. Nash was grateful for that.

"I don't think I want to clean him here," Uriah said. "Slick as it is, I might slip and open myself up. We'll take him back on top and gut him there."

The deer was a full-bodied three point, and heavy. Uriah and Nash each grabbed an antler, lunging, skidding and falling toward the top of the hill a step at a time. Sometimes they slipped, and their work of the past ten or fifteen minutes would be lost as they tumbled downward with the deer, a mass of legs, bodies, elbows, and antlers.

It was hard work, and before long, both Uriah and Nash were gasping, sweat dripping off their faces to the snow below. When they were within twenty feet of the top, Uriah stopped, blowing like a winded horse.

In speech broken by long struggles to fill his tortured lungs with air, Uriah said, "Go up. Throw down a rope. Nell can pull him . . . the rest of the way."

Nash scrambled to the top on leaden legs and tender feet, breath coming in short gasps. He threw one end of the rope to Uriah and tied the other to his saddle. Uriah dropped a loop over the buck's antlers. Then he grabbed the rope, holding the buck's head up while Nell pulled deer and man to the top.

Uriah stood for a long moment, hands on knees, gasping, before kneeling beside the buck, knife in hand. The gutting went quickly, and Nash helped his father clean the cavity with handfuls of snow, until the snow came away white.

"Getting late," Uriah said, scrubbing his hands with

snow. "We better get back. It's not far. We'll just drag the deer and skin him there."

Flynn flagged them down at the edge of the camp. He was carrying a rifle, and Uriah knew Flynn was worried, or he wouldn't have dragged the old buffalo gun out from its hiding place.

"Nice buck," Flynn said.

"Right where you said he'd be," Uriah answered. "Any trouble?"

"Nope. Real quiet. Guess I'm just getting old and suspicious. On the other hand, maybe I got old *because* I'm suspicious," Flynn said with a grin.

"You know, for a little help with the skinning and butchering, you could have some loin steak tonight that would probably make you sorry you ever ate anything else."

"For a couple of loin steaks, I just might do that."

Nash dragged the deer next to the tree where they had hung the sack of meat from the doe just a few days before. He dropped the carcass there, and walked Nell back to the corral, returning a moment later for the roan.

Flynn and Uriah cut the deer's legs off at the first joint, breaking them over their knees like sticks of wood. Then they skinned the lower section of each hind leg, leaving the main tendons at the back of the leg exposed. Flynn took a pine branch a couple inches in diameter and shoved it through the loops made by the tendons and bones of each hind leg. Then Flynn and Uriah tied a rope to the middle of the stick and hoisted the deer toward a low-hanging branch, while Nash took up the rope's slack from the other side.

"Nice heavy deer," Flynn said, breathing deeply from the effort.

Then, beginning with the hind legs, each man began tugging the hide off the deer, using their knives occasionally when the skin clung stubbornly to the meat. When the hide was loose from the carcass and draped over the deer's head, Uriah took out his knife again, sawing away at the deer's neck until the head and hide fell to the ground.

Nash took the hide, being careful to hold it by the hair so he wouldn't be forced to touch the slick, sticky side of the skin, and dragged it over to the trees, where he hung it over a protruding branch. When he came back, Flynn was bent over the deer's head. Nash waited until Flynn was finished. Then he carried the deer's head, its opaque, blue eyes staring at nothing, and a bloody hole where the animal's mouth had been—Flynn liked deer tongue for sandwiches—to the trees too. He didn't know why he felt compelled to throw the head out of sight. Perhaps he never would.

As Nash walked up, Flynn and Uriah were deftly carving away the slab of tenderloin that lay on either side of the backbone between the ribs and the haunch. Nash glanced up the hill some two hundred feet away. The old man was still there, wrapped in his robe and watching them, but still Nash was surprised at what he saw.

"Dad," he said softly. "The old man's drinking whiskey."

Uriah looked up, but the bottle was hidden under the robe again. "Funny. Somehow, I didn't take him for a drinker."

"Whiskey!" Flynn spat. "Would have been a kinder thing to have killed them all rather than given them whiskey." But Flynn couldn't hold his anger, not with the prospect of those steaks on his mind. His face crinkled into a reluctant grin.

"On the other hand, I have just a wee bit more, and I don't think it would hurt us at all."

"I'll take you up on that," Uriah said, reaching for the pint Flynn pulled from inside his jacket. "Nash, you go up and invite the old man for dinner. We're going to have to figure some way to get him out of here when we leave."

Nash walked toward the old man, stepping high to carve a path through the virgin snow that lay between the corral and the old man's camp.

No fire, Nash thought. How can that old man sit outside on a day like this without a fire?

Nash sat down across from the old man on the rock he had used in each of his earlier visits. He waited for the old man to speak. When he didn't, Nash did.

"Dad wants to know if you want to come to dinner. We've got some more liver."

Nash's invitation died when the figure sitting across from him leapt across the dead fire pit and caught Nash by the neck. Bullsnake! Bullsnake had been sitting under the old man's robe. Bullsnake's fingers were cutting into Nash's windpipe, and he couldn't breathe. He had both hands on Bullsnake's wrist, trying to push the hand away from his throat, but he wasn't strong enough. He was too dizzy and weak. He could barely hear the words Bullsnake was hissing in his ear. "I'm going to teach you not to laugh at your betters, boy. It's going to be a lesson you'll never forget."

And then Nash was falling. The snow took him in the face like a glass of ice-cold water, and he started breathing again, holding his burning throat in his hands.

Uriah was there. Nash didn't know where Uriah had come from, but all at once, he was there. As Nash's mind cleared, he realized that it wasn't his father at all. It was that creature with the opaque eyes his father had become when he was shoeing Nell. That creature was stalking across the campsite.

Bullsnake was saying something. Nash couldn't make it out, but the creature paid no attention. He just kept coming, and the smirk in Bullsnake's face turned to concern and then to fear. Bullsnake launched a roundhouse swing at the creature's chin, but the creature flicked the punch aside like a pesky fly. . . . Like a pesky fly.

It was years ago. Nash and his father had been sitting in the tack shed where Uriah was mending harness. It was one of those quiet days of fall. The harvest was in, and it was almost as though the farm had taken a deep sigh of relief.

Nash was playing step-and-fetch-it with his father. "Nash, get me that awl over there on the end of that shelf. No, no, son. The top shelf. . . . How about taking some oil and working it into this harness? That would be a big help."

Nash was enjoying himself. He liked the quiet, the smell of leather and oil and horse, the time with his father, the feeling of pulling his weight, the talk.

"You take care of your things, and your things will

take care of you. Doing this now will save us—*"us"*—a lot of time next spring."

They sat there together at the rough wood bench, worn smooth by tools and harness and elbows and hands.

Outside, the air was fresh as the scent of an apple orchard in spring, and bright and clear as it is at no other time of the year. The sun was lingering, sorry, it seemed, to leave the farm for the winter.

But the shed was dim, lit only by streams of light squeezing through cracks in the door and walls. Flies, big blue flies, had come to the shed for warmth the night before and were now buzzing about in the dim light. Uriah hung the oiled harness on the wall and then turned. Like the sun, he seemed reluctant to leave. His eyes drifted through the rays of light and caught on a fly buzzing about, looking for a place to lay its eggs and die.

And then Uriah's hand moved, moved faster than Nash believed anything could move. It flicked into a circle of light and snapped the fly out of the air. "Pesky damn flies," Uriah said, dropping the crushed insect to the floor.

"You pick up in here, Nash, and when you're done, come inside. I think I might have a piece of stick candy stashed in there someplace."

But Nash seemed preoccupied. "I'll be in in a minute."

Uriah left the shed door open a bit as he stepped out, pausing for a moment to look back through the crack. Nash was standing in the middle of the little room, his fist darting out toward the flies and coming back empty.

"Pesky damn flies," Nash said, and Uriah smiled as he walked toward the house.

Pesky damn flies. Uriah's hand snatched a fly off the point of Bullsnake's nose—once, twice, three times. Bullsnake's head snapped back until it seemed he had seen something terribly interesting in the sky directly overhead, as though he were unaware of the stream of blood that sprayed out of his nose like water coming off a drainpipe in a gully washer. He might have been out on his feet then, but his face pitched forward and down. Uriah's fist—driven by arm, shoulder, back, hip, and leg—met it on the way down, and Bullsnake's neck snapped back again. His legs buckled and he crashed to the ground, lying motionless there.

Uriah pounced on the fallen man, pinning him to the ground, and then Uriah's right fist moved back behind his shoulder. Nash knew that his father was cocking the fist. He knew that his father was going to beat Bullsnake to death. He knew, but he couldn't speak, couldn't move. He felt as though he were in a dream, watching what was happening without being a part of it. He knew he was watching his father beat a man to death, and he could do nothing.

But the killing blows didn't come.

Uriah looked up, and the opacity of his eyes fled like frost from a window on a warm winter morning. Nash knew it would be all right. His father had beaten the creature in a fair fight.

Still Uriah sat there, fist cocked simply because his rational mind had not yet reminded him to drop it. It was then that Uriah and Nash heard the ugly *snick* of a rifle hammer going on full cock and Flynn's voice, low and deadly. "I saw a man shot with a Sharps once. It damn near cut him in half."

Uriah turned very slowly. Maxwell was crouched behind him with a long ugly knife held low and menacing in his right hand. And behind Maxwell stood Flynn, cradling a cocked Sharps rifle in his left arm. The unwavering muzzle, pointed square at the back of Maxwell's head, belied Flynn's look of a man absolutely at ease.

"If I were you, Maxwell," Flynn continued in the same voice, "I'd drop that knife."

Maxwell stood for a long moment without moving. Then he spoke. "Did you kill him?"

"No," Uriah said.

Maxwell eased out of his crouch and dropped his knife, the snow muffling the sound of its falling.

"He ain't a bad kid. It's just that he can't keep his mouth shut."

Maxwell walked over and knelt by Bullsnake, holding a handful of snow against the bridge of his nose to stop the bleeding. When the snow touched Bullsnake's face, he groaned.

"What happened to the old man?" Flynn asked.

"Bullsnake scared him off. Didn't rough him up or nothing. I told him that I wouldn't stand for that."

"How far do you think an old man like that will get in weather like this without even a robe to keep him warm?"

"He's an injun. He might make it."

"And if he doesn't?"

Maxwell shrugged.

"It doesn't make much difference to you one way or another, does it?" Flynn asked as he walked up, easing the hammer down on his Sharps.

Maxwell shrugged again.

"If he dies," Flynn said, "some folks might think that you and your mouthy friend helped him along a little."

"He's an injun."

"What the hell does that mean?"

"Where are you going to find a jury who will hang a white man for kicking a freeloading old Indian out of camp?"

Flynn sighed. "I want you two gone by first light tomorrow. I'm going to keep your weapons, including that knife. Next time somebody from the ranch goes into Billings, he can drop 'em off at the Stockman."

By this time, Bullsnake had rolled over and was rocking dizzily on his hands and knees. He got up in stages, and it was clear to the watchers that everything he did for a while would be painful.

His eyes rolled when he looked at Uriah.

"Keep dad crazy sub-of-a-bidge away frob me. He tried to kill me!"

But the opaque-eyed creature had gone, maybe for good. Uriah had beaten his own personal devil in a fair fight, and when he spoke, his voice had no challenge in it.

"Which way did he go?"

Bullsnake had expected a sharp pointed boot in the ribs. Had he come out on top, that's what Uriah would have gotten. But Bullsnake was put off balance by the absence of malice, triumph, hate, or fear in Uriah's voice.

Bullsnake's relief was reflected in his quick reply. "Ober dad hill."

Then Bullsnake staggered off with Maxwell toward their camp, his arm over Maxwell's shoulder.

Uriah looked at Flynn. "I'm sorry that happened. I didn't mean it to."

"Sometimes it can't be helped."

"Dad, we've got to go get the old man, or he'll freeze to death."

"It's almost dark, Nash. By the time we get a quarter mile the sun will be down."

"If it was me out there, would you come looking?"

"Sure, but—"

Flynn chimed in again. "You two go ahead. I'll get the fire stoked up and the steaks ready for fryin'. When I see you coming back over the top, I'll throw them in the pan."

"Better walk," Uriah said. "By the time we get over to the corral and get the horses saddled, it'll be dark."

The trail was clear enough. The old man had walked almost straight up the hill. Nash noticed one spot where he had slipped and fallen, picked himself up, and started climbing again. Once the old man reached the top, his stride lengthened, and it was clear he had been making good time.

Nash and Uriah followed easily until the trail dipped behind a small stand of juniper. The track led into the stand of tangled, gnarled wood, dead and alive, and disappeared. Uriah and Nash spent the rest of the light looking through that little stand of juniper, but the old man was nowhere to be seen.

Nash was the first to speak. "We might as well go back. We aren't going to catch him tonight."

Uriah paused. "Nash, you can't really believe that old man's story. He can no more 'run on the wind' than I can. He probably backtracked and followed somebody else's tracks until he was free of camp. Age has stolen his mind, Nash. Nothing more. Nothing less."

Nash nodded. Had it not been for the tenderness of his toes, the walk back to camp would have been pleasant. It was still cold, but the night was bright with the reflection of starlight off the snow.

Uriah pretended to be otherwise occupied, but Nash could see that he was watching every step the old man had taken from the camp. Uriah was trying to find a sign that the old man had backtracked, some indication where he had stepped off the trail. Nash knew his father was wasting his time.

11

It was still dark when they awoke. Neither felt much like eating, and they left camp just as the false dawn was settling into the hills. Neither talked about what direction to take, despite Uriah's insistence the night before that the old man had backtracked.

They followed his tracks out to the juniper bush and beyond, holding to the direction the old man had set from camp. They didn't talk. There didn't seem to be anything to say. They were bound on the old man's course now, and both felt compelled to follow it to its end. The sun had just touched the eastern horizon when they came to a coulee. The walls were steep, too steep to take a horse down. Uriah scanned the coulee up and down as far as he could see. There were no tracks there, no reason to believe there had ever been life in the coulee beyond the heavy juniper and pine growth hanging on its edges.

"Nash, I think we're wasting our time. I think the old man backtracked last night. I think he found himself a hole and pulled it in after him. But I know that you will never feel easy if you don't try to find him. You take the shotgun and drop down into the coulee. I'll take the horses around the head of it and follow down the other side. You walk along the bottom until you find an easy way up. We'll meet up at the top on the other end. If we haven't found some sign of him by then, Nash, chances are we'll never see him again."

Nash slipped off Nell, handed the reins to Uriah, and started walking toward the edge, carrying the shotgun in his right hand.

Uriah threw him a handful of buckshot loads. He caught all but one, and he bent over to pick it up after he stuffed the others into his pockets. He broke open the shotgun, blew snow off the cartridge, and dropped it into the chamber. He pulled another shell from his pocket, loaded it, and snapped the action shut.

Nash walked up to the edge, picking his way down the slope with his eyes before stepping off. He could hike to that juniper bush there, catch a branch and brake himself.

From there, it would be relatively easy to ease down to the rock outcropping, catching his breath there before moving on.

Taking a good grip on the shotgun, Nash stepped out on the slick surface of the slope leading to the coulee floor. He was slipping and sliding, trying to keep his own balance. He sped toward the bottom. Nash grabbed a juniper branch in passing, and it held. He clung there for a few moments, searching for his next handhold. He reached the rock outcropping without incident, and from there it was a relatively easy leg to the coulee floor.

Nash walked carefully up the coulee, taking care not to snap a branch beneath his feet, to conceal himself as best he could while he walked. He was hunting now, simply because it was natural for him to move that way in the winter, with a gun pulling hard against his right shoulder. He didn't really expect to see any animals. He didn't really expect to see the old man. Somehow he knew whatever part he and his father had played in that strange old man's life was over.

Still, Nash trudged along the coulee quietly, enjoying a day made brisk and not bitter by a cold winter sun hanging over the edge of the coulee.

He had just turned a bend in the coulee when he saw the rabbit. It came out of the juniper bush tentatively, moving toward Nash, toward another bush that hugged a rock outcropping at the bottom of the coulee. Better cover there, Nash thought. And then it came to him. The rabbit was moving toward him! Something up the coulee had frightened the animal.

Nash's eyes examined the coulee, seeking movement

in shadow, seeking a profile against the backdrop of snow. His eyes moved over it first and then back again.

It was the wolf! It was *the* wolf! Flynn was right. There was no mistaking this animal, no more than the sound of a rattlesnake could ever be mistaken for anything else.

He stood across the coulee, quartering toward Nash and absolutely magnificent. He was huge, with a black band across his eyes, and Nash was suddenly reminded that the old man had told him black was the Cheyenne color of death. Nash knew root deep this was the animal they had been hunting, but still his mind wrestled with that knowledge. This wolf was obviously in its prime. It couldn't be as old as the wolf that killed ol' Charley. . . . That killed ol' Charley.

And then Nash's reflection was replaced by fear.

The eyes. Flynn had talked about the eyes. They were green, as green as Flynn had said and deep . . . so deep . . .

It was a hot summer afternoon, and Nash had abandoned his hoeing in the garden and walked down to the big deep hole in the creek. He shed his clothes, climbing naked to a big branch of cottonwood tree overhanging the water. Then, savoring the chill as the waters closed over his head, he swam. It was green, sun-drenched jade green at the top and darker as he struggled through the water to the bottom of the hole. He swam against the current, trying to reach the head of the pool before he ran out of strength, ran out of air. He was about halfway when it came to him that he wouldn't make it, and when he looked up at the mirror reflection of the surface above, he knew he wouldn't make that either. It was too far away, and his tortured lungs would overcome his brain. He would suck water instead of air, and he would cough himself to death, trapped in that deep green pool.

The wolf took his eyes from Nash, and the boy gasped for air, realizing for the first time that he had been holding his breath, caught in the depths of that wolf's eyes. He stood gasping for a moment before it occurred to him to raise the shotgun. Nash slipped back both hammers to full cock. The wolf was watching the rabbit now, but he made no move toward it or toward Nash. Nash's finger tightened on the trigger. *"Squeeze don't pull."*

But the finger stopped, still in place but motionless. Nash was thinking about the old man, about the stories he had told about this magic wolf. He remembered the wonder in the old man's voice as he spoke about the medicine lodge where the spirit wolf had revealed his secrets to a young Cheyenne boy.

He remembered Uriah talking about how badly they needed an irrigation ditch if they were to survive the Montana summers, remembered the watermelon he watered every day, only to drop it on the way to the house. He remembered his mother sitting at the piano, wringing her hands and weeping softly.

The weight of the barrel was pulling the muzzle down away from the wolf. Nash let the barrel drop. He took a deep breath and another, trying to quiet the pounding of his heart. Still the wolf didn't move. The animal's attention was focused up the hill behind him. Nash raised his shotgun again.

Ka-whump!

The shotgun reared against his shoulder, and Nash stepped back against the recoil. Then he looked up the hill where the wolf had been. The animal had slipped to the bottom of the coulee. It lay there, green eyes open, but without magic.

Nash let down the other hammer of the shotgun. He was standing motionless as Uriah came around a distant bend in the coulee, the roan scrambling to keep his footing in the snow. Uriah pulled up and jumped down. "You okay?"

Nash nodded.

Uriah levered a cartridge into his rifle and walked toward the wolf, holding the rifle to his shoulder, the muzzle on the animal. Uriah reached out, prodding the wolf with the barrel of his rifle before kneeling to examine it.

"Looks like we're going to have to do a little more target practice. You only hit him with one pellet, right in the temple."

Nash walked over to the animal. "Look, Dad. His fang is missing, just like Flynn said. It's the wolf, isn't it, Dad?"

"It's the wolf. There's no way in hell there can be two animals like this around. How'd you run across him?"

"It was almost like he was waiting for us. He just stood there. He didn't move, except to look up on the ridge there behind him."

"Well, we'll get a chance to see what he was looking at. We'll have to take the roan up that side coulee to get out. No way we'll ever get up what I just rode down."

"Why do you suppose he just stood there like that, Dad?"

"Nash, you know enough about animals to know that they don't think. He wasn't waiting. You just caught him by surprise. Maybe he was listening to me and the horse and didn't even know you were coming until you got there."

"I think he knew."

"I think you're making something out of nothing. Next thing you know, you'll be figuring there's some connection between this wolf and that old man. Don't let your imagination get away from you."

The roan shied a bit from the extra load and the smell of wolf, but Uriah gave him a boot in the ribs and the horse settled into the task. The side coulee was broad and gentle, and it was obvious from the number of tracks that animals used it regularly. It forked near the top, leaving a point of rock directly ahead of them. Uriah took the left fork, angling toward the top. A few minutes later, they topped out. Uriah pulled the roan to a stop, looking over the land below so that all the details would be clear in the telling and retelling of the hunt.

"Dad! Look at that!"

Nash was pointing to the little rock promontory overlooking the valley below. Just back from the edge of the rock was an Indian burial scaffold, and on the scaffold was the old man.

Uriah and Nash climbed down, Uriah taking the old man's buffalo robe from behind the saddle.

The old man lay on his back on the scaffold, his arms

hugging his chest as though for warmth. His eyes were closed, just a sliver of black and white showing beneath the lids. But there was no glitter there now. The magic had left his body. He seemed older than he had in life, and infinitely fragile.

Uriah picked up the old man as though he were a child, holding him in his arms while Nash spread the robe, hair side up, on the platform. Then Uriah lay the body gently on the robe, folding it over and tying it with leather thongs from his saddlebag.

"That will keep the magpies out of his eyes. I don't know how to do this," Uriah continued, and Nash wasn't sure whether his father was talking to him or to Wolf Runs on the Wind. "But I will do the best I can."

Uriah took off his hat, waiting for Nash to follow his lead. Then he bowed his head and closed his eyes.

"Lord, you know I'm not much for praying, but I'm asking you to listen to me now. This old man couldn't help being what he was any more than a coyote can help barking at the moon. And I don't pretend to know Your scheme of things, so maybe he was just what You wanted him to be. That's something between You and him. Anyway, I ask You to give him the benefit of the doubt. Amen."

Nash echoed the "amen," hesitating a moment before laying the old man's knife on the burial scaffold.

"I don't really need it, Dad."

Uriah nodded. They donned their hats and climbed aboard the waiting roan. Nash felt a sense of loss over the old man's death, but no sorrow. The old man had come to the hunt with this end in mind. Nash was convinced of that. Maybe he was where he wanted to be, running on the wind with the spirit wolf at his side. Wherever he was, he wasn't on the scaffold any more than an old pair of boots was the man who had worn them.

Uriah and Nash rode in near silence for some time, the only sounds the creak of leather and the muffled thumps as the roan's feet hit the ground. Then Nash spoke.

"He was still warm, wasn't he, Dad?"

Uriah nodded.

"How do you suppose he knew to wait there? How did he know to build the scaffold there?"

"It was just a coincidence," Uriah said. "Just a coincidence."

Nash nodded. There was no reason to debate the point.

Center Point Publishing
600 Brooks Road ● PO Box 1
Thorndike ME 04986-0001 USA

(207) 568-3717

US & Canada:
1 800 929-9108